CHARLIE WELLS WAS DIGGING HIS OWN GRAVE...

It wasn't a truly proper grave, six feet deep, not in that rocky mountain soil. But it would cover a man. And it was deep enough for them to climb down into—nearly three feet—and then see who was going to climb out alive.

They agreed on Bowie knives.

"Now!" Wells cried, and charged his antagonist. The next moment in a flash of knives Charlie Wells dropped with his blood swelling out of the great gash in his guts. A second slash opened his throat, and the man who had argued with Riot McTeague lay in his last resting place.

Charlie Wells wasn't the first man killed by Riot McTeague. Nor would he be the last.

Also in THE GUNSMITH series

MACKLIN'S WOMEN
THE CHINESE GUNMAN
THE WOMAN HUNT
THE GUNS OF ABILENE
THREE GUNS FOR GLORY
LEADTOWN
THE LONGHORN WAR
QUANAH'S REVENGE
HEAVYWEIGHT GUN
HIGH NOON AT LANCASTER
BANDIDO BLOOD
THE DODGE CITY GANG
SASQUATCH HUNT
BULLETS AND BALLOTS
THE RIVERBOAT GANG
KILLER GRIZZLY
NORTH OF THE BORDER
EAGLE'S GAP
CHINATOWN HELL
THE PANHANDLE SEARCH
WILDCAT ROUNDUP
THE PONDEROSA WAR
TROUBLE RIDES A FAST HORSE
DYNAMITE JUSTICE
THE POSSE
NIGHT OF THE GILA
THE BOUNTY WOMEN
BLACK PEARL SALOON
GUNDOWN IN PARADISE
KING OF THE BORDER
THE EL PASO SALT WAR
THE TEN PINES KILLER
HELL WITH A PISTOL
THE WYOMING CATTLE KILL
THE GOLDEN HORSEMAN
THE SCARLET GUN
NAVAHO DEVIL
WILD BILL'S GHOST
THE MINER'S SHOWDOWN
ARCHER'S REVENGE
SHOWDOWN IN RATON
WHEN LEGENDS MEET

CROSSFIRE MOUNTAIN
THE DEADLY HEALER
THE TRAIL DRIVE WAR
GERONIMO'S TRAIL
THE COMSTOCK GOLD FRAUD
BOOMTOWN KILLER
TEXAS TRACKDOWN
THE FAST DRAW LEAGUE
SHOWDOWN IN RIO MALO
OUTLAW TRAIL
HOMESTEADER GUNS
FIVE CARD DEATH
TRAILDRIVE TO MONTANA
TRIAL BY FIRE
THE OLD WHISTLER GANG
DAUGHTER OF GOLD
APACHE GOLD
PLAINS MURDER
DEADLY MEMORIES
THE NEVADA TIMBER WAR
NEW MEXICO SHOWDOWN
BARBED WIRE AND BULLETS
DEATH EXPRESS
WHEN LEGENDS DIE
SIX-GUN JUSTICE
MUSTANG HUNTERS
TEXAS RANSOM
VENGEANCE TOWN
WINNER TAKE ALL
MESSAGE FROM A DEAD MAN
RIDE FOR VENGEANCE
THE TAKERSVILLE SHOOT
BLOOD ON THE LAND
SIX-GUN SHOWDOWN
MISSISSIPPI MASSACRE
THE ARIZONA TRIANGLE
BROTHERS OF THE GUN
THE STAGECOACH THIEVES
JUDGMENT AT FIRECREEK
DEAD MAN'S JURY
HANDS OF THE STRANGLER
NEVADA DEATH TRAP

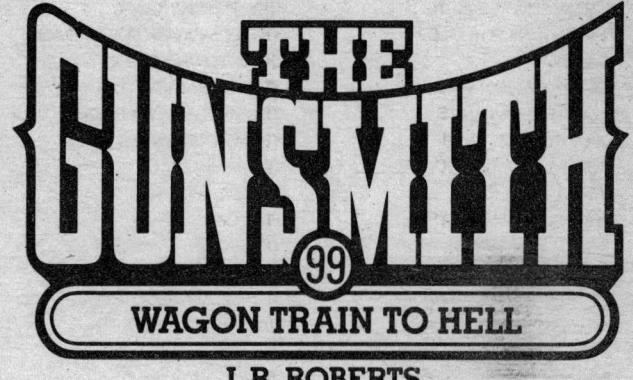

WAGON TRAIN TO HELL

J. R. ROBERTS

JOVE BOOKS, NEW YORK

WAGON TRAIN TO HELL

A Jove Book published by arrangement with
the author

PRINTING HISTORY
Jove edition/March 1990

All rights reserved.
Copyright © 1990 by J. R. Roberts.
This book may not be reproduced in whole or in part,
by mimeograph or any other means, without permission.
For information address: The Berkley Publishing Group,
200 Madison Avenue, New York, New York 10016.

ISBN: 0-515-10272-5

Jove Books are published by The Berkley Publishing Group,
200 Madison Avenue, New York, New York 10016.
The name "Jove" and the "J" logo
are trademarks belonging to Jove Publications, Inc.

PRINTED IN THE UNITED STATES OF AMERICA

10 9 8 7 6 5 4 3 2 1

ONE

From the lip of the high canyon wall Clint Adams looked down on the sway-backed prairie schooners standing in a circle, pole to chain-gate, the customary defensive position in the face of Indian attack. He saw the dead horse but nothing that looked like dead bodies of the defenders. Still, he was far away and he had only that moment come upon the scene, called by the sound of brisk rifle fire.

It appeared to be a small band that had attacked the wagons, and the hostiles had clearly drawn back. The Gunsmith realized it was not a major confrontation and supposed it had been a renegade band or maybe simply some young warriors, tired of reservation life and hungry for action. He knew the Sioux were at peace with the whites—according to what he'd been told back at Fort Stanton.

It wasn't a big train, only eleven wagons, yet it

was clear to the Gunsmith that the men were well armed. It had sounded like the wagon-train men had Spencers. The weapons would be enough to repel just about any Indian attack, even when the defenders were greatly outnumbered. Clearly, the whites had beaten off the hostiles in the present action.

Now, through his field glasses, the Gunsmith studied the scene carefully, covering the ground for some distance around the circle of wagons, then looking across the river for sign of the Sioux returning.

Then he saw the column of seven near-naked horsemen, their skin burnished in the bright sunlight that bore down from the pinnacle of the sky as they rode out from a large stand of box elders on the far bank of the Little Wood River. At a signal from their leader, they kicked their ponies in the direction of the high benchland that broke across his view to the west and north leading toward the Wapiti Mountains. Obviously they had swiftly realized the potency of those Spencers and had decided the risk was too great.

Clint brought his glasses back to the wagons again and watched the men talking and gesticulating around the short man with the big hat and what looked like fancy clothes—he seemed to be some kind of leader.

He looked back at the Indians who were now almost out of view. They weren't hurrying and were clearly not expecting any pursuit. Suddenly he felt uneasy. Something was off about the whole action. The hostiles had given up too easily. True, there were those Spencers, but they hadn't even attempted to go against them, or so it appeared. He wasn't quite sure, and it was hard to tell at that distance; but he felt that something was not right. Yes, they just seemed too casual—something like that—as they rode away. But he put it out of his mind as he slipped the glasses back into their case, then checked the big black gelding's rigging and mounted.

He had left his gunsmithing wagon and the team of bays a short distance away, under cover. The bays were cropping the thick bunch grass when he rode up now on Duke. One of them tossed his head to look at the man and horse approaching, then bent again to the tawny-colored grass; the other kicked at a deer fly somewhere on his belly but didn't stop chomping, while his harnass jingled and now his bridle as he shook his head vigorously against the pesky flies.

Clint dismounted, removed Duke's bridle, and slipped a halter over his head before tying him to the end-gate of the wagon. He climbed into the wagon seat with the lines in his hand, then slapped leather across each bay's rump, clicking his tongue at the same time.

A while later, as he approached the wagons, which were now lining up before pulling out, he noticed someone waving at him. He thought it strange that only one person waved, although he could see that the others were aware of his arrival. And again he felt that strange feeling that there was something odd going on. There didn't appear to be all that agitation that was usually associated with a narrow escape from an Indian fight. And while he certainly didn't expect a brass-band greeting from the members of the wagon train, he didn't feel the sense of relief and welcome that would usually have been forthcoming. Yet the feeling was vague. People often acted strangely after going through a confrontation with the Sioux.

The men had been lining up their wagons, and now most of them stopped as the Gunsmith approached. The short man with the big hat whom he had seen through the glasses began walking toward him, accompanied by two large men who looked very much alike.

"Welcome, stranger!" The voice under that big Texas hat boomed forth, and Clint noted the flash of a gold tooth.

He drew rein as the three men came closer, and now he saw that the two younger men were identical. Twins. Big, with big, broad shoulders, big hands, big heads. Bulls, the Gunsmith decided, and something told him they were a definite part of the person that the man in the middle, the man with the huge hat and gold smile, chose to turn toward the world. They looked like twin buttes, Clint decided. Tall, wide, immovable, and with just as little expression on their faces. Looking at them, he felt something stir inside him. A memory? He couldn't place it. There was no time for searching his memory now; he knew that. He knew that he needed everything he was; and right here, right now, in this moment.

He sat there at ease on the wagon box as the three men had to turn their heads upward to see him. Indeed, he hadn't stepped down on purpose, wanting them to do just that—have to look up at him.

Yet, in spite of the presence of the Twin Buttes, as he called them in his mind—their size, their force, their obvious aggression—his attention was more interested in the man standing between them.

"Name here is Joseph Stillox, sir. My companions here are Clancy and Nole Hooligan. We're mighty glad to see you!" He had a long, thick, pitted nose and very big teeth.

Clint nodded, wrapping his lines around the brake pole but still not climbing down. "I'm Clint Adams. Saw your wagons from the top of the canyon yonder, but I see you didn't need much backup."

"Didn't need any," said the one named Nole Hooligan, almost grunting the words.

His twin brother nodded, and something appeared in his face that Clint Adams took to be a grin. He saw now that each had a bulge beneath his coat, which only seemed an obvious addition to their aggressive presence, as he studied them again and more closely.

"Know what kind of Injuns they were?" Stillox asked.

"Sioux. You're on their land. Likely that's why they confronted you. They say what they wanted?"

Stillox was sucking his teeth loudly, as though his tongue were chasing after a piece of food lodged uncomfortably someplace or other. "Beef, booze—who knows?" But his attention was really on his search, and finally he won out, prying the offending piece of food out with his fingernail.

Clint noticed that the nail was on his little finger and that it was longer and more pointed than its companions. It fitted with his yellow silk shirt, black broadcloth coat, gray trousers, Wellington boots, his black string tie and also the diamond ring on the same hand as the fingernail. He thought it interesting that Stillox was so obvious about his weaponry, including the twin behemoths standing beside him. It had to be a role, he decided. Yes, indeed, the clothes, the whole demeanor was fancy, as he'd thought when he first spotted him through the field glasses. Clint realized he was looking at an accomplished bunco artist, at the least.

"Step down, sir," Stillox was saying. "Join us for victuals. Perhaps a drink of something—coffee? Or possibly something more invigorating, eh?" And a big chuckle rumbled up from his belly and popped out of his mouth. Clint spotted another gold tooth.

A group had formed, and most of the people were staring at the Gunsmith, though when he looked back they looked away.

"Folks, we'll be moving on. We don't know if those wily redskins will bedevil us again or not. In the event, we are ready. Clancy and Nole and myself, and our trusty weapons, will protect us all." And Joseph Stillox beamed at the gathering. "Move along now!" And, still beaming, he made a sweeping gesture with his hands, as though urging little children off to bed.

He played the role admirably, Clint realized as he followed Stillox to his Conestoga, with the twins bringing up the rear at a distance.

When they were alone inside Stillox's wagon, his host brought out what looked like a good bottle of whiskey—definitely not trail stuff. He poured into two mugs.

The twins were evidently waiting outside. Clint could almost feel their presence.

"You look to me like you know this country, Adams. That so?" And Stillox cocked his head and an engaging eye at his guest, with a smile just touching the corner of his mouth.

"I've ridden it before," Clint said. "I know it some, though that's a while back. I'd say a good while." He was looking right at the other man, holding his gaze steady. And for a period of several seconds neither moved. Clint was determined to stare the man down. He knew Stillox had worked the situation toward this struggle of wills. And he knew, too, he could have easily looked away and just as easily kept on staring at him. But Stillox was clearly trying to settle something with him, and the Gunsmith was by no means going to let him have his way.

Suddenly Stillox looked away, smiling. "We've lost our scout, Adams. So we're—well, we're not too sure just where we are. I'm hoping you might give us a hand."

"Where are you heading?"

"Oregon. Except if we find a good place to settle, well, we might stop there. Most of us, I'd say, are looking for a new home, a new life. The Great West has called us!" He opened his arms, as though greeting the sun.

They were each seated on buffalo robes, and Clint noted that his host lived well. There were quite a few robes in the wagon and weapons, though he saw no Spencer. He counted two Henrys, a Remington, and seven holstered handguns hanging at one end of the wagon. Clint also felt a woman's presence in the cozy quarters.

"We'll be moving out very soon, Adams. I do wish you'd stay with us. Help us."

At that point the flap of the wagon was pulled back and one of the twins entered, followed by his brother. Clint realized he couldn't tell them apart. He wondered if Stillox could.

"Ready to move out," the man who had entered first said. He looked over at Clint. "Amelia's fixed you some grub, case you be hungry."

"Thanks," Clint said. "I'll wait till the rest of you eat. Besides, it'd be good to get out of here now. We don't want them coming back."

"And finding us here," Stillox said with a grin. "Though we would certainly give them what for!" And he chuckled, looking at each twin in turn and then at the Gunsmith. And then he added, his tone soft with piety, "Us and the Good Lord."

"Amen," said the twins in unison.

Clint looked at the three of them impassively, swiftly taking in this fresh view of his hosts.

Stillox resumed, a smile on his face, his hands folded together in his lap: "I have a feeling from the sound of your voice, Adams, that you might ride along with us a way. Am I correct?"

The man was surely engaging. Clint had to hand him that. "I'll give it a try," he said. "That is—for a way. I'm not going very far in your direction, but I'll help you out, Mr. Stillox."

His three companions grinned at him, and Clint felt a definite change in the atmosphere inside the covered wagon.

And then Stillox said, smooth and simple as a wafer, "I neglected to tell you, Adams: it's not 'mister'; I happen to be a reverend."

TWO

He was glad to finally get away from Stillox's wagon. But the time spent there had been rewarding. Toward the end of their meeting they had talked about which way they would take to be sure they would not run into any more Sioux. And yet, all the time they were talking, Clint felt something false about the conversation. He said nothing of this, but he fed Stillox and the twins to get whatever information he could for his own use.

He had told them he was heading north for Willow Crossing and that he could scout for the wagon train that far. After that they'd have to be on their own, or they'd have to find somebody if they planned to continue "toward Oregon."

Someone had brought coffee then and they talked for maybe half an hour longer.

He asked Stillox how he had lost his scout.

The reverend seemed to take a deep breath, and he looked quickly at his two companions before responding. "He was a man we picked up when we stopped over at Laramie. Man name of Burroughs. Hank Burroughs. Came with a recommendation, I can't remember whose. Do you boys recollect?" He threw a glance at the twins.

Neither said anything to that but only shook their heads, almost in unison, Clint noted.

Stillox continued: "He 'peared to be a top man. Worked hard. Didn't drink, didn't do anything to suggest he wasn't right on the up-and-up. Then 'bout a week later he suddenly up and took off."

"Took off?" Clint Adams cocked an eye at each of the three men in turn as he said those two words.

One of the twins picked it up then: "Back at a place called Widow's Gulch. We stopped for water, for the horses." He had spoken suddenly, Clint thought, like someone who suddenly realizes it's his turn. "It was back at Laramie we heard talk of Injuns up ahead. Hostiles, some said. Others said they wasn't. But we were glad to meet up with somebody who knew the country."

"We didn't want to take any chances," Stillox said. "So we asked around about getting some scout or someone who knew the country—like that. And that's how we wound up with Burroughs."

Stillox paused and was about to go on, but the other twin cut in: "It was just after dark when we seen Burroughs wasn't with us. We saw too that his horse was gone, plus his bag and bedding." He spread his big hands, a strange smile on his face, and his big shoulders rose and dropped in a shrug.

Stillox was nodding in agreement as the twin concluded what he had to say. "That was the way of it."

"And there was no sign of why or how?" Clint asked.

"Well, see, it was dark by then," Stillox said. "So we couldn't see much; had better luck in the morning."

"There was his pony tracks leading north," one of the twins said.

"Not back the way you'd come, then," said Clint.

"Right. And we followed them, me an' Clancy, until they gived out at a creek."

"Walked his hoss into the water," Stillox put in. "An old Injun trick I bin told, huh, Nole?"

"That's what I heared," the twin named Nole said.

Clint was studying the two of them to see how to tell them apart. And then he thought he had it. But all three of them were looking at him, expecting him to say something.

"And did you question the people in the wagons? I reckon you must have," Clint said.

"We questioned 'em," the Reverend Stillox said, speaking slowly, as though reading the words, and in a bad light to boot, Clint thought. He wondered suddenly if all three had been drinking. But the thought passed as he bent his attention to what Stillox was saying.

"We—I—questioned them," Stillox said. "But nobody had heard or seen a thing. Nothing! Can you beat that!"

"But had Burroughs been acting strangely or had anybody noticed anything different about him since he'd been with the wagon train?" Clint asked.

"Nope!" Nole Hooligan brought the word in hard. "Man just up an' dee-cided to haul ass!"

"And leave us in the lurch with those heathen redskins," intoned Stillox in his church voice. His face was long, and his eyes moved dolefully upward.

But Clint Adams had caught the whine in the voice and had the distinct feeling that Stillox was acting.

"So then, if I can get you to Willow Crossing, I figure you'll be able to pick up a scout without too much trouble. And maybe by then, if you study the lay of the land, and learn a couple of things, you might not need any scout. At least for a ways."

"Maybe Willow Crossing would..." Clancy started to say, but then he caught himself and cut the sentence off.

Clint was pretty sure Clancy had almost put his foot in it but had suddenly remembered something. At least he must have felt the poke brother Nole jabbed into his side.

And then, just as he was putting down his empty coffee mug, Clint remembered how he had definitely heard the sounds of more than one Spencer just before the Indians took off.

At the same time, he knew that the Spencers had been issued only to certain units of the U.S. Army and that no one—no private person—had such a weapon. Nor—supposedly—did any Indian.

He was looking at Stillox's hands as he thought this. They were not the hands of a man who toiled with the plough or axe, nor were they those of a man who worked cattle. They were thin, even slender, and again Clint noticed the long, pointed nail on the little finger of the reverend's left hand. He'd seen nails like that on professional gamblers.

Now, riding into the late afternoon as the sun was

dropping toward the horizon—swiftly, it seemed—he was enjoying the fresh air away from Stillox's confining quarters. And a good thing it was, he told himself. For he wanted to think.

The impressions had been so many and at the same time were so loaded with warning that he really needed to spend time sorting things out.

First of all, there was Stillox. The man was clearly not at all as he appeared. The role he was playing was quite transparent. He was like a second-rate actor who hadn't taken the trouble to study his part or learn his lines.

Not for a minute did the Gunsmith believe that the man was traveling to Oregon, nor that he and the members of the wagon train were looking for a place to settle and begin new lives. Nor did he believe the strange account of how their scout had left them.

It was when they had pulled into a circle at a campsite he had picked for them that he again noted something even more interesting. As evening fell and campfires were lighted, Clint saw again that with the exception of himself, Stillox, and the twins, no one with the wagon train was packing a gun, neither a handgun nor a rifle. And he only knew about the weapons carried by Stillox and the Hooligan brothers because he'd spotted the tell-tale bulges under their coats.

"Victuals," as the Reverend Stillox, put it, were important as "the time when folks get together." And indeed, the members of the train all supped in one large group that evening. Yet there wasn't much talking. A few remarks were passed about the Indian trouble, but other than that there was little of what

Clint Adams would have called fun and laughter. Some of the younger children played, but they were warned by the twins not to stray from the camp circle.

Guards had been posted, and a night watch with shifts was worked out. The men on guard duty were issued Henry rifles, but not handguns, by the twins.

"Had a little gun trouble after we left Laramie," Stillox explained. "Somebody horsing around with another man's wife got shot in infraction of the Lord's Rule." He sniffed, all the way up his long nose, and spat. "Bastard got his, by damnit!"

"You're saying he got killed," Clint said.

"He better be in that condition, on account of if he wakes up or comes to he's gonna have a helluva time getting out of that hole the boys planted him in." And the reverend shook with uncontrollable laughter at his little joke.

Wiping his eyes with the back of his wrist, he resumed his conversation by observing that he had a good feeling about having Clint along as scout.

"The others feel that too," he said, lowering his voice. "See, that's why I took away their guns. Can't have trouble like that when you're crossing this big country with all its dangers just lying in wait for ya."

"You say you don't have any particular place in mind to settle, if I understand you," Clint said.

"That is so." He cleared his throat, which was loose with phlegm, looked about for a place to spit, and then finally let fly at a wagon wheel. "Oughtta grease that axle, by God," he muttered. "Nothing like good ole spittle to get things movin'. You watch how a farmer, he'll take an' spit on his hands 'fore he handles that shovel or hoe, or whatever. Same with a man fixin' to cut up firewood or fell a big timber. He'll salivate on his palms so's he gets a right good holt on that axe. Same principle, see!"

By now the women were cleaning up, and someone had brought out a banjo and was starting to strum on it.

"Better keep that low," one of the twins called out.

"How do you tell those two apart?" Clint asked. "They sure look like they came from the same pea pod."

Stillox's face widened into a grin, which grew bigger and bigger. "Thing is, Adams..." But he couldn't go on. Laughter overtook him, and he fell into near hysterics, almost falling off the box he was sitting on, and, indeed, popping a button on his fly from the severe gyrations his body took to accommodate the violent attack of mirth that broke through him.

Finally, his breath sawing as he dabbed his knuckles into his streaming eyes, he gasped out, "Don't matter. See, them boys are like the same. One is just as dumb as th'other. You tell one somethin' it don't matter, he'd do it just like his brother. Neither the one nor th'other got a thought of his own." He managed to recover himself finally, and he continued in a more sober tone.

"I got 'em when they was real young. I mean, small! Orphans, they were. I took 'em in, placed them under the wing of the Lord." His big eyes rolled to the sky above, and a somewhat heavenly sigh shook his small though sturdy body. "They never do anything alone, see, Adams. Therefore, they ain't gonna think alone. Hell, I do believe they don't even take a leak alone. Now, what you think of that? What would two persons like that do out in the big wide, cruel world without the other? Hell, man, I mean, without me. Without Joseph Stillox, man of God!"

His—for Clint—lengthy declamation ended on a sepulchral tone, and again his eyes rolled heavenward. He mopped his brow with the sleeve of his coat, and a sigh ran through him.

"I need to know what kind of guns you have, Stillox, if you want me to scout this train for you, I've got to know what I'm handling here. How many men, women; what they're like, who can do what, and how much you've got for weapons."

"Of course, of course, Adams. I understand that. How about in the morning, when it's daylight and everyone can be called together?"

"Now," Clint said firmly. "The Sioux could be back, and we'd be up the creek for sure. I don't notice anybody here who can handle a full-scale attack."

"We held them off before, Adams!" Stillox said sternly, his chest pushing out, his face reddening as he blustered and sniffed angrily. "You got no right to—"

"Then you do your own scouting, mister."

"But you agreed. And we don't know the country!"

"Look, those Indians weren't even half trying. If you couldn't see that, then you're blind. Let's cut the shit and get down to it. I heard Spencers in that fighting. Where are they? Who's got 'em? You know, half the army of the west would give their eye teeth to have that weapon. Did those Indians have

Spencers? If so, how come they were driven off? Or did you have them? And if so, where are they? Stillox, I need to know. We are in a tough spot here. Those Sioux could be back. They could bring their friends with them. Now then, if you want to talk straight to me, start right now. If not, we'll forget it."

The reverend had changed his tactics completely. He was all at once soft, open, friendly. His voice was muted, and his gestures seemed to embrace the air in front of him as he wove his thin hands in explanation and apology for having "seemed ornery."

"Adams, we—I, too—have been under a big strain. We have a lot of people here who don't know a gun from a plough. And there are women and children. Well, you've seen them. They are God-fearing men and women, and they say their prayers. You can take my word for it! I've led them in prayer. And now I am responsible for them, and since Burroughs left us, we realize what kind of a logjam we got here. Believe you me. But . . ." And he held out his palms, offering. "I will do whatever you recommend. I just thought that in the morning it might be better, but we'll go through it right now."

Without further ado, he raised his voice and began calling the wagon-train people together.

When they were all gathered, Stillox addressed them. "Folks, as you already know, Clint Adams here is going to be our scout—at least for a good piece of the journey—and we can thank our lucky stars for that. Now, you listen to Adams here!"

At that point he turned to Clint. "Tell 'em what you want, Adams." And at just that moment the Gunsmith caught him looking over at one of the twins as he added, "We will back whatever decisions you make."

Clint stepped forward. He could see Amelia, the woman who had handed him his grub tools at supper, standing at the edge of the group. He hadn't had a good look at her before, because his attention at the time had been on something one of the twins had been saying to him. And now his view wasn't any too clear, for the woman was standing between a big beefy man smoking a pipe and an old woman leaning on a cane, who was unsteady to the point that the young woman had to reach out and take her arm. It occurred to him that she had to be Stillox's woman.

"The Sioux might come back, and they might not," he said. "In any case, they will likely figure us to pull out tonight. Except I see some of your teams need rest. And also, we don't have to do just what the Indians expect. So we'll move out in early dawn. Meanwhile, I want you to show me what weapons you have."

A long, silent pause followed his words, and he was about to speak again when one of the twins, at a nod from Stillox, spoke.

"I'll fill you on that," he said.

Clint turned to Stillox. "That right? He knows?"

"That's right. He's got a list of all the weapons."

"I want to see that list."

Stillox nodded and turned toward his wagon. "Come on in. You boys, too. This needs to be private."

When they were inside the Conestoga, one of the twins handed a list of the train members to Clint.

"Who wrote this?" he asked.

"I did," said the twin, who happened to be Clancy.

"No you didn't," the Gunsmith replied.

"Say..." Both Hooligans spoke in unison, while the one named Clancy reddened, and at the same moment Clint Adams saw his brother, Nole, coloring.

"Take it slow, boys," Stillox cautioned. "Now, why do you say that, Adams?"

"You calling us a liar?" Nole said, speaking for the first time in hours, it seemed to Clint.

"I'm telling you that neither of you know how to write that clearly, if at all," the Gunsmith said. He turned to the reverend. "I thought the horseshit was out, Stillox." And he stood up to leave.

"No, wait a minute. Wait! Please wait!" Stillox rose too, hitting his head on one of the bows supporting the canvas roof of the Conestoga and cursing. "Adams, they didn't write it, but they have custody. See, that's what was really meant."

Clint looked at the Twin Buttes, who had remained seated. Each had the same malevolent stare on his face.

Clint realized he was asking for trouble, but he saw no point in continuing the game on the Stillox-Hooligan terms. "I want to know who owns what gun or guns and where those guns are. Plus what ammo they have. And I don't want any more bullshit with any of you. Do it my way—get it?—or skin you own horses to wherever the hell you're going."

"Agreed!" said Stillox, glaring at the twins. "Fully agreed!"

"Good enough." The Gunsmith stood up, but he had to remain bent so his head wouldn't hit the canvas. "We'll be pulling out before dawn. I want to see the men now armed with their own guns, and I want to see them lined up outside." He threw his thumb over his shoulder. "Right now! I want to see those guns, the ammo, and I want to see the men with them." He pointed to the bulge inside Clancy Hooligan's coat. "Including all of yours. You might think you can pull this kind of shit in some half-assed saloon town, but out here on the trail it's serious business. And you better not forget it!" He started to step outside but turned back. "I'll scout you as far as Willow Crossing, like I said. And then we'll be quit of each other. Meanwhile, we will do things my way or not at all."

Stepping down from the Conestoga, he saw that some men were standing in a small group near the wagon.

"You men looking for me?" he asked.

One of the group, a man wearing a red bandanna under his black Stetson, was about to speak, but at that point one of the twins stepped down from the Conestoga and dropped to the ground. He was followed by his brother.

Nobody said anything then. The twins looked at the group of men, all of whom turned and walked away. Clint waited a moment while the twins walked off in another direction. In the near distance he saw a woman lifting a child into one of the wagons as the twins approached. They walked by without looking to right or left, and presently there was hardly anybody about.

Clint lit a cigarette, striking the Lucifer on the bottom of his thigh. He heard a sound in the wagon behind him and, turning, saw Stillox appear and sit down in the driver's seat.

"Sorry for the misunderstanding, Adams. We're all under the gun here. And like I told you, them two"—and he nodded his head in the direction the twins had taken—"ain't exactly bright. And they sometimes got a tight bit in their mouth, if you figure what I mean."

"I see that," Clint said. "But I don't aim to make them my problem."

The reverend chuckled. "Leave them my problem, then? Hah! Well, I took 'em on as a work of the Lord. And I will continue to offer them guidance, as I will these." And he spread his hands out wide, palms up, sweeping the wagon train. "Let us face it, Adams. It was the love of the Lord that saved us from those wild Indians!"

"Could be," Clint admitted. "But could be, too, that those Spencers did some helping," he said meaningfully.

Twenty minutes later the men were lined up outside their wagons and the twins had distributed their guns among them.

"You men keep those weapons clean and in good operating order. I'll be inspecting them in the morning. It's late now, so it's up to each one of you to take care of your weapons. Remember, your own life plus someone else's can depend on that."

When he was through, he took a look at the pair of Spencers the twins showed him.

"This it? Only two?"

"That's it," one said. Clint was still not able to tell them apart, though since they dressed slightly differently he was able to know, once he had established the correct name.

"You're saying there are only two of these here?" he asked, bulleting each one of them in turn with his eyes.

"That's right." It was Nole speaking.

Clancy added, "That is right."

He didn't believe it. And by the way he intentionally looked at each one in turn, and then looked at Stillox, they knew he didn't believe it. That was his intention.

The men had dispersed now, most of them going back into their wagons. Three remained standing by the dying cook fire, talking in low tones—evidently about their weapons, it seemed to the Gunsmith, judging by the way they were pointing to them.

"Goodnight, Adams. God be with you." Stillox paused, as though studying something—trying to remember a part, Clint thought, watching him.

"I'll take a look around before I turn in, check the sentries, and ride up ahead a bit. There's still fair light to see by," Clint said.

"And to be seen!" said Stillox. "Just be careful that you make yourself known. We don't want any accidents."

And with that parting admonition, he nodded and disappeared into his wagon.

Clint had already decided where he would throw his bedroll, and now he walked over to his gunsmithing wagon and lifted it out of the box and carried it to a stand of bullberry bushes and willow a good distance from the edge of the camp. He put it down but didn't unroll it. He squatted near it, listening, getting used to the early night noises. He was wondering why there had been no casualties during the fight with the Indians. Only the horse, and that had been an accident, one of the twins told him. A member of the wagon train had shot him by mistake. But Clint was wondering why—with Spencers and with some vigorous men in the party he had seen at supper— why, then, had no one managed to hit even one of the attackers?

But he didn't dwell on the question. After a minute or two, he stood up and picked up the bedroll. He moved it about twenty feet away and spread it just inside the line of willows, from where he could command a view of anyone approaching across the small clearing. Then he stuffed clothes into it to make it seem that someone was lying there. He waited, hunkered down, and smoked a cigarette, making sure that the smell of tobacco was well into the immediate atmosphere, so that it could be detected by a sharp nose.

He stayed there, listening. After a while he drew back into the willows and moved around to the other side of the clearing. He found a likely place with a clear view, which also offered protection for himself.

He waited.

He had made himself a makeshift bedding some yards away from the dummy figure, with a clear view of anyone approaching across the small area of buffalo grass and with a fair view along the edge of the timber. For a while he remained standing just inside the trees, and afterwards he knelt down, resting, then sat crosslegged, changing his position every so often in order not only to avoid stiffening but to keep fully awake.

He judged a couple of hours had passed when he heard the snap in the timber to his right, close to the dummy bedding. Instantly he was alert. He had been sitting crosslegged, and now without a sound he rose to his feet, his right hand close to his six-gun.

When he saw the figure moving toward his bedroll he didn't change his position but simply waited. He watched. He was sure it wasn't one of the twins; the figure was not big enough. But he didn't think it was Stillox. He saw the figure moving, then suddenly stop; obviously, whoever it was had discovered there was no one there and that the bedroll had been stuffed.

But the Gunsmith didn't show himself. It could easily be a trap, with someone else covering the man by the bedding, should he challenge him. The figure all at once straightened up, and he saw that it was a woman. She was small, and he wondered if she were one of the women who had cooked supper. There was sufficient light for him to see that she was not one of the older women; he could tell by the way she moved. He wondered if it were Amelia, Stillox's woman—a plain, though not unattractive, person. If so, would she not be acting as a decoy for him to put himself on target?

"Hello?" the voice was soft, compelling, but he could hear the fear in it. He knew it was not Amelia.

Clint decided to take a chance and released a soft, low whistle between his teeth. She started, turning in his direction, and he had the feeling that she was young and intelligent—afraid, yes, but also she must have courage, for she was taking a chance. Or was she? Was she maybe setting him up?

"Over here," he said softly, and then quickly,

soundlessly, he moved away from his position.

Now, from several feet away, he watched her come toward the spot from which he had called her.

"Mr. Adams?" Her voice was just above a whisper as she entered the line of trees in which he had been standing only a few minutes before and which he now had covered with his Winchester. At the same time, he had a full view of the clearing she had crossed.

Nothing.

"Mr. Adams, can I talk to you? I am alone. I was sitting by Amelia at supper when she was getting your things for you. I'm Molly Durham. There is no one with me. No one knows I'm here."

Clint allowed a beat and then he said, "Over here," moving again as he said it and watching her approach. Yes, he half recognized her now as she came close. And now she stood inside the line of trees. The light coming through the tops of the trees was good enough for him to see the outlines of her face and body. He verified what he'd thought earlier: that she was young—he guessed under thirty. And he could feel her energy as strong, with nothing of the dispiritedness that some of the other members of the wagon train seemed to have.

"I'm sorry to barge in on you like this, Mr. Adams. But... but I felt I had to."

"Don't be sorry. Just tell me what's on your mind."

"It's—it's that I heard some men talking and it worried me. They were talking about going to 'get' you—I believe they used that word—except I'm not exactly sure what they were saying, now that I'm trying to tell it to you. I... I guess I really had a feeling about it more than anything else, anything—actual. Am I making any sense to you?"

He had caught the agitation in her voice instantly, and at the same time he realized that she was no flibbertigibbet caught in imagined fear. There was something about her he definitely admired, and it wasn't only the strong sense of her sexuality that was holding him almost like a hand. Clint Adams was not a man to be swayed by sexual feelings in a moment when a cool head was required. At the same time, he fully realized that this woman's strong sexuality was a definite part of her strong character. He could hardly make out her features in the night light, or her figure, and yet he still felt something drawing him but by no means overwhelming him.

"Molly..." He said the name as though listening to it.

"Yes."

"Do you know who the men were? And are you sure they were intending to do me harm, or was it just that they planned to keep an eye on me?"

"I can't swear to it, but I do think from the way they were talking—the sound of it, you understand—that they were not just intending to watch you. I felt it, but I cannot prove it, that they wanted to do something bad."

"And who?"

"I think one of them was one of the twins, but I can't tell them apart."

"And who else?"

"I don't know. Maybe the other twin."

"What else?"

"They were standing by one of the wagons as I

walked past on the other side. I didn't particularly want to hear them, only I couldn't help it."

"Did they see you?"

"I don't know. But they might have. Mr. Adams, there's something about that wagon train. Something strange. And I must say it worries me."

He said nothing, and she moved closer to him. He could smell her, feel the strength of her: a quiet, very female strength.

"Do you understand what I'm saying?" she asked.

"I do. Tell me, has anything happened to you while you've been with the train? Anybody tried to harm you or threaten you?"

She shook her head. "No. Nothing like that. It's just—well, like the air or something. And I've asked myself, is it my imagination? Like that man who was the scout—he just suddenly disappeared. Why? What happened to him?"

"They told me he just rode off without telling anyone."

"But why would he? He was a nice man. He was serious. But he was also jolly. But did you see any of those people smile? I haven't seen them happy since we left Laramie. And why did they take everybody's gun away?"

She was looking down, her hands hanging at her sides. Then she looked directly at him. "I am sorry. I shouldn't have taken your time like this. I—please forgive me. I just . . . I just felt you might be in danger, too."

"Do you think you are?" he asked suddenly.

She hesitated only a moment. "I don't know. Except that I have a feeling that maybe all of us are in some kind of danger. I don't know why I feel that. Of course, I... well, there is Mr. Stillox. And those twins. They're strange! And since you ask, I don't like the way they look at some of the younger women, even the young girls." And then she added quickly, "Please don't get me wrong, Mr. Adams, I'm not an old maid who is against—well, against carnal feelings, if I could put it that way. But those men are... well, *spooky* is the word."

"Have they bothered you?" Clint asked. "I mean, in that way?"

"No, no. Nothing like that."

"But you must have a husband," he said quickly, gently.

"My husband is dead."

"I am sorry."

She was standing very straight before him, with her hands together at her waist. "He was shot and killed—murdered—in Laramie just two weeks before the wagon train left." She stopped, her head dropping as she looked down at the ground. He could feel her breathing heavily. "He—Mitchell—was shot in the back. I wasn't there at the time; it was in a saloon or someplace like that. The verdict was given as self-defense, so the murderer of my husband was allowed to go free."

"You mean there was a trial?"

She shook her head. "No. The verdict was given by the town marshal, on the spot. There was no arrest, no trial; only the body of my husband to be buried. Which I did."

She raised her head. "I ask your forgiveness for telling you all this. I am sorry. I have not said it to anyone else except a little to Mr. Hildebrand, whose wagon I joined, along with an older couple and a widow and daughter." She seemed to square her shoulders then as she looked right at him. The night sky was still bright, and he thought he saw tears standing in her eyes. "Mr. Adams, I have indulged myself in speaking to you like this, and I apologize. But I really did feel those men might try to do you harm."

"I appreciate it," Clint said simply.

"I just want to say one thing more: I did not love my husband. We were friends, but I was not in love with him. But that—terrible thing—should not have happened to him." She paused. "I guess I got carried away," she went on, looking down again. "I only wanted to warn you."

And now she turned away, but he reached out and touched her arm.

"That still doesn't tell me why you joined the wagon train," he said.

"I believe I've spoken enough. Once again, I do apologize."

"But you're leaving me hanging here," Clint said. "There's a reason why you joined the wagon train. Did you just want to get away from Laramie? Was that it?"

She seemed to be turning something over in her mind, for she was silent for a long moment. When she spoke again, her voice was almost a whisper, though he could still feel the strength in her words.

"Yes, I wanted to get away. I can't tell you how much, how very, very much, I wanted to get away."

"But why the wagon train? You could have taken

a stage out of town. And there's the railroad. Why Stillox's wagon train?"

"Because I believe the man who killed my husband is with us. I don't know who he is. I haven't the least thought of who he might be. But I am sure: I know he is traveling with the wagon train."

THREE

In the early predawn the camp was fully awake. And before the tip of the sun had touched the horizon, the wagons were lined up and ready to move out. Clint had conferred with Stillox. Except for his encounter with Molly Durham, the night had been uneventful. Yet he experienced once again the feeling that he'd had when he first encountered the Stillox wagon train. And so he was open to the girl's story. As he rode out again to take the lead, he saw her sitting next to the driver of the last wagon, to which he had tied his team. She looked toward him but made no sign. Nor did he. The man beside her had to be Hildebrand, then, the man who had come up to him early on and offered to take care of his team and gunsmithing wagon while he was riding point and scouting.

Yet he had a good moment seeing her more fully

in daylight, and in light of what she had told him he realized that she had to be under great strain. She was courageous. Yet he wondered if she understood what she was up against. If it were Stillox and the twins, it would be no easy matter. If it were one of the members of the train, well, she could take her pick. For she had told him just before leaving the night before that she didn't know what the man looked like or even what name he'd be traveling under.

He was happy to be riding point, away from Stillox and the twins—or anyone else, for that matter. He wanted to think, and he also wanted to have his entire attention on the work at hand. They were still in Sioux country, and it was still possible that they might hear again from the band that had attacked them.

He had gambled on not moving the wagon train during the night. The Sioux would have expected that the wagons try to escape. The point was that Clint was pretty sure the Indians were gone, on the one hand. On the other, if they were going to launch another attack, the site the train was in right now was as good a place as any to fight them off.

Glad that his hunch had proven correct, he still did not relax his vigilance as he rode on well ahead of the wagons, looking for signs, estimating likely places for an attack, figuring how much ground the wagon train could cover in the kind of terrain they were traveling over.

They were well into the rugged Bear Tooth Mountains of the Absaroka range. It was a while since he'd last ridden that country, but the memories came back; even though, being a good trailsman, he didn't let himself rely on memory. Memory could be faulty, and what was more, what might have been thoroughly familiar for years could change and throw a man off, to his peril.

In any event, he had heard that Willow Crossing was a town that was growing. Growth could mean good news to a gunsmith, for where there were people there had to be guns. And guns needed a good smith to work them, to repair them, and, as Clint Adams surely more than any other gunsmith of his time and place had to know, to shoot them, if necessary.

But at that moment Clint Adams was riding his big black gelding Duke into the Bear Tooth Mountains toward Willow Crossing, and he had no idea in what strange form the action in which he would shortly be involved was going to take place. Nor did he have a notion of the very strange villain-hero-showman he was going to encounter.

One summer afternoon, not very long before the Gunsmith and the strange wagon train he was guiding entered the Wapiti Valley, two Wyoming cattlemen rode up to a thin body of water known as Bullberry Creek and dismounted their horses. Each had carried to this lonely spot a pick and shovel, which they untied, and now they began to dig.

They had put their gunbelts aside and had also taken off their shirts. In only a few moments they were digging in rhythm with each other, their shoulders, backs, and chests shining with sweat.

Above them an eagle swept the intense cobalt sky, and though they didn't know it, a coyote had paused carefully, not very far away, to watch them.

Both diggers were big men, both powerful; both carried a determination that was obviously not to be denied. One was a man named Riot McTeague, a hairy man wearing his black hair down to his shoulders, in the old Indian-fighter style. His black beard accentuated the vigorous blue of his eyes. He was just over six teet tall, with long, powerful arms, yet with thin, tapering fingers.

His companion was huge, with a barrel chest, hamlike hands, and he was maybe an inch shorter than McTeague, yet wider—a buffalo of a man who handled his shovel as though it were a spoon. His name was Charlie Wells.

McTeague paused to rest on his spade and wiped the sweat from his forehead.

"Come on," said Wells. "Don't dog it. You got to dig as much as me." There was no anger in his voice; it was as though he were speaking casually to a friend.

McTeague smiled. "Reckon I'll be digging more than you by the time we're done with this here," he said. "That ought to even her."

Charlie Wells looked at his companion but without any expression on his face, nor did he stop digging.

Meanwhile, the sun burned down from the high sky as the two men picked and hacked and dug their way into the soil.

"It's one helluva place to dig a grave," Wells said after a while, when they both stopped again to rest.

"Won't be bothered out here is the idea."

His companion nodded and resumed digging. And after a while, the digging was easier. And finally it was done.

"Well, it ain't regulation," McTeague said,

scratching into his thick black beard, "but it oughtta do. I reckon you'll be comfortable in it."

Charlie Wells spat indolently at a clod of hardpan that he had just shoveled out of the trench. "Since you're thinner than me, you'll be right snug in there, my friend."

McTeague grinned. It wasn't a truly proper grave: six feet deep; not in that hard, rocky mountain soil. But it would cover a man, and the length and width —eight feet by four—was right. And it was deep enough for them to climb down into it—nearly three feet—and then see who was going to climb out alive.

It had been McTeague's idea. He had been arguing with Wells about rangeland and water rights, and he suspected running iron activity for over a year. The situation had built to bullet talk, and McTeague had seized the initiative and suggested the duel be held in a grave. And his adversary had agreed, supposing that he were probably the stronger man physically. In fact, they were evenly matched, though it began to be evident now that McTeague was the more confident.

"Are you breathed?" he asked Wells.

"Reckon. Yourself?"

"Let's get 'er done with, then."

They had agreed on Bowie knives, which each had brought along. And now each stepped carefully into the grave. For a tight moment they stood staring at each other in silence, perhaps listening to their own breathing. They had decided that there would be two signals. McTeague would give the first, and both of them would squat at each end of the grave. Wells would give the second signal, and the fight would begin.

"Now!" The word snapped out of Riot McTeague, and both men squatted, their eyes fixed on each other, their knives ready, each muscle alerted to the word that would fire them into action.

McTeague's idea had actually come from a gunman he had heard about and admired: the Texan Clay Allison who had fought another man over water rights in this fashion. Allison had lived to tell about it; his opponent had not. And now McTeague planned to do the same as that fabled Texas gunman. It was even better—more different—than a handkerchief fight—each man holding onto the same handkerchief and fighting with knives until one was finished. He had been surprised that Wells had agreed. And pleased. Riot McTeague was a man who had always liked drama, the unique, the big gesture.

Right now each man was concentrated only on the action before him. Nothing else existed; not even the reason for fighting. Not even one's own life.

The sun burned down on them.

"Now!" Wells cried, and he charged his antagonist.

The next moment, in a flash of knives, Charlie Wells dropped with his blood swelling out of the great gash in his stomach. A second slash opened his throat, and the man who had argued with Riot McTeague lay in his last resting place.

McTeague was a considerate man, and now as he finished filling in the grave he stood bareheaded and said a prayer—to a man whose courage he admired, though not his folly at attempting to best Riot McTeague.

Charlie Wells had by no means been the first man killed by Riot McTeague. Nor—as the victor was wont to promise those who were within earshot—would he be the last.

"Our road is clear now," McTeague said one morning as he awoke in bed with his friend Angie.

Angie's red hair tumbled across her face as she raised herself up on one elbow to look at her companion. But since her mass of hair was completely covering her vision, she started to swear.

Chuckling, McTeague rolled toward her and parted her thick red hair with his fingers to look into her indignant green eyes.

"Don't you let a lady have some privacy, mister? Who do you think you are?" And, having delivered herself in this fashion, she stuck out her tongue.

Quick as a wink, her companion leaned forward to bite it but missed, whereupon she kneed him none too gently in the crotch, though taking care not to damage anything.

Then they both succumbed to laughter, tickling, and, inevitably, another round of lovemaking.

Later, he watched her covertly as she rose and walked naked to the mirror above the bureau, there to admire her own curvaceous figure. She regarded herself head on, then from each side, looked at her behind, and then faced herself again with her hands under her large and buoyant breasts.

McTeague ogled her from the tangled, sweaty sheets. "C'mere."

She spun around and stood sway-hipped, one hand holding up a breast, the other holding up her mop of red hair.

"Wot's on yer mind, podner?" she drawled, Texas fashion. "Like as if ah didn't know!" And without warning, she charged across the room and leaped on top of him.

The bed crashed to the floor, the brass posts falling away and one crashing into the bureau. But this delayed the lovers not at all. She was on top of him with his rigid weapon high and deep into her.

"God almighty!" she moaned. "You're hitting my belly button with that thing."

"I haven't even started yet," he gasped, as his loins pumped in unison with hers and she spread her legs wider.

In the next moment he had flipped her over onto her back and was now stroking in a deep, long, slow rhythm, bringing his member almost out, teasingly to the very edge of her vagina, and then sliding it in deep and hard. Then, moving it faster as she kept perfect time with him, they went faster and faster and faster... until neither could see, hear, think—could do nothing but be totally claimed by their exquisite passion as together they came and came and came.

He had dozed off but was suddenly startled awake.

"What the hell you doin'!" he demanded, rubbing his left buttock. "You pinched me, damnit!"

"I didn't pinch you. I pulled out one of the hairs on your hairy ass."

"What the hell for! You crazy or somethin'!"

"I've been doing it each time. Is this the first you've noticed?"

He sat up and looked down at her, lying there with her face buried partially in the pillow. One green eye was mischievously showing.

"I thought something funny was going on the last couple of times," he said. "Jesus Christ! What the hell are you doin' pulling the hairs on my ass!"

"I only pulled one at a time, honey." She cooed softly and snuggled closer to him.

"What for, for Christ sake!"

"I just wanted to keep score," she whispered.

"Keep score!"

"Yeah. I think we broke our record this time."

He lay back down, sighing and muttering.

"My ass is hurting," he said. "That's a helluva way to show your love for me."

She raised herself up on an elbow then as he lay back on his pillow. "This bed is crazy," she said.

And indeed the bed was tilted, so that their heads were lower than their feet, the foot of the bed being propped up on the bureau.

"Listen, you green-eyed wildcat, my butt is sore from all that hair pulling."

She was still leaning on an elbow, looking down at him. She gave him an air-kiss then and pouted a little as she said, "Then I'll just have to kiss him better. Turn over."

Refreshed, Riot McTeague came pounding down the stairs into the barroom of the Inside Straight Saloon & Gaming Parlor & Dance Palace. The big handsome sign outside the establishment announced the title in full, but no one—not even Riot McTeague himself—had ever been heard to utter it in its entirety. At least nobody cold sober.

This morning, as was his custom after he had stayed the night in one of the upstairs rooms— usually Angie's—McTeague ordered coffee, steak and spuds, and sourdough biscuits. Then, on second thought, he added flapjacks. He felt particularly good, not only after his bout with Angie, but because of events.

"Events are falling in," he told One-Eye Gallagher, his manager at the Inside Straight, as he drank his coffee and lighted his first cigar of the day.

"Good to hear that," One-Eye said. "You bin sayin' they would, Riot, an' I know how you is mostly right about things."

Fortunately, Riot McTeague was in a good humor. "What do ya mean, 'mostly right'?" he demanded, frowning at Gallagher.

But One-Eye was neither slow nor stupid; he had gauged his employer's humor—as he almost always did—just right. "*All* the time," he said, relenting majestically with a sweep of his hands, rolling his good eye heavenward in mock prayer while the glass orb stared solemnly nowhere.

McTeague chuckled, scratching into his thick beard and sighing as he exhaled a cloud of cigar smoke.

Chrome, the bartender, had arrived with the food and with a cup of coffee for One-Eye, who was considered by the staff to be McTeague's right hand. Which he was, but only in town. At the outfit, the Double Bar Cross, up by Tall Horse canyon, McTeague's other hand was L. T. Moses, a name open to much funning, though not in the presence of L. T. McTeague, to be sure, was the exception. He not only funned Moses about his name and his ten commandments but revealed the caliber of his wit in such remarks to One-Eye Gallagher as asking which eye One-Eye was wearing on a particular day—the left or the right. McTeague was famous for his funning. He was also famous—need it be said?—for his reaction should any ignoramus make the mistake of trying to fun *him*.

When the door had closed behind Chrome, and the smell of steak and potatoes mixed with cigar smoke, McTeague beamed up on the man seated across from him.

"I have word—got it last night—that Stillox is on his way. Also that the operation went smoothly."

"Smoothly?" One-Eye's eyebrows shot to his hairline as he scratched his bony chest and looked at McTeague's left ear, where the lobe had been chewed away in a passage at fisticuffs, which the chewer had lost. "Why, I heared otherways."

"You are referring to the unexpected company they now have?" McTeague said smoothly.

"I am. Feller name of Adams. Never heared of him." One-Eye turned his good eye closely on McTeague, who was rapidly devouring his breakfast with much gusto.

"I have heard of him," McTeague said. "I was speaking of the Spencers." But he spoke with his mouth full, and his companion had a hard time making out what he was saying.

"Huh," said One-Eye. This was always a more or less safe form of ejaculation when the boss spoke incoherently, either from eating while talking, or chewing on his cigar, or engaging in some other physical interruption such as belching. One-Eye, and indeed all those who remained in Riot McTeague's service, were always mindful of their employer's limited amount of patience. A person might ask once what the boss said, but never twice. And even asking once was permitted only with veterans such as One-Eye, who had the good sense not to overwork the privilege. Like now, offering only the simple ejaculation "Huh."

"Clint Adams. He is otherwise known as the Gunsmith."

"Him!" One-Eye's jaw dropped at the same time that his dry lips pursed in a mixture of surprise and awe. And for a minute Riot McTeague thought—and even hoped—that he would drop his glass eye, which he had once. But he was disappointed.

"What luck!" McTeague said, now attacking another thick, juicy chunk of steak. "Imagine that feller turning up at a time like this!"

"Boy, you don't 'pear to mind one bit. You know, he's quicker'n a cat on a greased pole with that six-gun of his!" One-Eye's mouth formed a silent "oh" to emphasize the Gunsmith's speed as a gunfighter.

"You think I should mind, do you?" McTeague said, his tone playful, as he threw a glance at the man on the other side of the round card table.

"Well, seems to me that feller, being what he is, could maybe upset things a bit."

"I reckon he could. I allow as how he could, my friend." McTeague wiped his mouth with the back of his wrist and the grin he turned on his companion reminded that man of a wolf. He'd seen that look before. He didn't like it. He was, in fact, afraid of it.

"I'm only sayin' we got to go careful," One-Eye said cautiously. "That man—uh!" He wagged his head, sniffed, and reached for his coffee.

"I look forward to the challenge," McTeague said brightly. "I like to size up them overstuffed gunfighters. You know, I might just take a notion to out-pistol the son-of-a-bitch, if I've a mind to. Or maybe just beat the shit out of him. But meanstwhile..." He leaned forward, his eyes on the drop of water that had suddenly appeared on the end of One-Eye's long nose. "Meanwhile, we will just see what he does." He leaned back. "Good to get some excitement into the action is the way I see things, you old fart. You men always want everything nice and smooth and easy. Hell, that ain't no fun. You want everything just like a cold-ass fuck, for Christ sake. What the hell good is that!"

One-Eye was suddenly grinning. When the boss was like this, you couldn't resist him. And, what was more, things always seemed to fall his way when he was in this mood. One-Eye laughed. "I get your drift. We'll watch him."

They were silent for a moment, then McTeague said, "I'll be heading out to the Double Bar in the morning. That wagon train will be a day or two more in getting here. You keep your eyes open while I'm gone. But, course I'll be here today. Got some things to wind up a bit."

"You riding out alone?" One-Eye asked.

"Don't worry about it." McTeague took a drag on his cigar, raising his head to blow the smoke toward the ceiling and watching it plume. "Now, I want you to watch that new faro mechanic.

"Stillman?"

"I believe that's his name."

"You seen something' funny about him, have you?" One-Eye felt the alarm cutting through him— maybe he had missed something important.

"And Pete. His eyes got bad or somethin'. He was using readers last night and fuckin' up. He come close to getting called by some waddie from that big cattle drive. What is it? The Quarter Circle HO, right? Yeah, maybe Pete needs a rest." He pushed back his chair and reached down suddenly and began scratching his leg. Straightening, his shoulder bumped the edge of the table, upsetting coffee. He ignored it and stood up.

"One-Eye, I want this whole place sharper. We got company coming, and I don't just mean the wagon train."

"You're meaning that Gunsmith feller?"

"Shit no! I'm talking about big, something real big! Big company! And we need to be real sharp, alert, ready. I mean, I don't want anybody like Pete Dinton fucking up with his readers, or that damn fool Krazewski almost tipping it that he's switching tops and flats. And that feller with that goosey way he's dealing faro last night. Hell, that dude, that English dude, he was like to spot him. He would have, by God, if I hadn't spilled my drink on the son-of-a-bitch. Jesus Christ! I can't trust a one of you. I better not go out to the outfit, or you'll let the place burn down, or some damned stupid thing. I can't trust a one of you! Not a one!"

One-Eye's good orb was filled with dismay as McTeague's mood changed. Oh, he knew it so well. One minute he was up, high as the sun; the next he was lower than fish shit. God! And when he was on one of these busts, then just watch the hell out!

McTeague, his mood totally reversed, stormed from the room at the back of the Inside Straight. One-Eye followed warily, careful to keep within earshot in case needed but not staying too close to attract unwanted attention.

Then he suddenly realized, as he saw his employer talking to Lew Manning, one of the poker dealers, that perhaps the boss had been putting it on, just in order to get some action going. He knew he did that sometimes. The trouble was, a man didn't always know which was which. But whatever or whichever it was, One-Eye dropped a long sigh all the way through his body when Riot McTeague finally left the premises.

FOUR

The sun was like a burning hand on his back. He could feel the heat through his boots, along with the dampness of his toes. His saddle horn was almost too hot to touch with his bare hand. As they rode, Duke gave off fumes that were acrid. His thick black neck was damp, but he kept his pace.

Clint Adams examined the horizon carefully, taking plenty of time, using the point of his hatbrim for positioning the land ahead. He studied all the sharp rocks, the rims, crags, edges, and lips of the volcanic formation of the mountain. He let his gaze swing slowly from side to side, seeing no riders, white or red. No one, then, watching from some crag or gully, peering over some hill or through timber.

The sky was clear as far as he could see. It was as if there was no air, only the endless blue, the rich, thick smell of sage, and his horse. Behind him the wagon train followed, the drivers hot and indolent as their eyes seemed only to follow the movements of their teams, while behind each, inside the Conestogas, the women and children occupied themselves one way or another.

The Gunsmith led them into a wide, rocky canyon at the end of the big strip of prairie they had just crossed. Here there was even less air, it seemed, and certainly no wind at all. Only heat waves. Red dust floated lazily upward as Duke's shod hooves pushed against the red ground that suddenly interrupted the rocky trail and then almost immediately gave out; now the shoes rang loudly on the rocky passage, and there were echoes singing back from the high walls.

A swiftly running creek bordered the trail now. He saw bluestem growing tall nearby. Higher up on a low bench, greasewood grew along with some spike cactus.

When he stopped Duke for a drink of water at the little stream, he thought of his bay team and gunsmith wagon hitched to the last Conestoga, looked after by the man named Hildebrand. Listening, he could hear the wagons entering the canyon.

He didn't wait for them but pushed on. Presently, as he and Duke broke out of the canyon and rode over a low lip of land, he heard a horse somewhere behind him. Turning in his saddle and leaning one hand on the cantle behind him, he saw one of the twins coming on a big sorrel horse with a wide white blaze. He was surprised to see him without his brother and realized this was the first time he'd seen the twins separated. He didn't slacken Duke's pace, however; he let the big man catch up with him.

"You push your horse like that in this kind of heat

you're gonna end up walkin' to wherever it is you're aiming for," Clint said sourly as the twin drew abreast on his sweating horse.

"Stillox sent me."

"You hear what I said about your horse? Long as I am scouting this wagon train, I expect all of you to take care of your mounts. You founder that animal, he'll be useless. You mind me?"

The twin grunted something that sounded to Clint like a grudging assent.

"First of all, tell me which twin you are."

"Clancy," the man said without looking at Clint and keeping his eyes straight ahead; he was obviously angry.

"That's what I thought."

Clint saw something like a smirk come into the corners of the other's mouth.

"Forgot. I ain't Clancy; I be Nole."

"That's what I thought," Clint said without any expression at all.

"You're pretty smart, Gunsmith."

"You're brighter than I thought if you understand that," Clint said. He was watching the other man closely out of the corner of his eye, holding Duke back so he wouldn't get too far ahead and he'd lose sight of Nole, or whichever one it was.

The twin said nothing now as they rode side by side.

The Gunsmith broke the silence, "What do you want? I'm riding point here and I got business to tend to."

"Mr. Stillox wants to know when we're going to hit some town."

"Tell him two days, like maybe the day after tomorrow, if we don't run into any Sioux, Arapaho, or maybe Cheyenne or Shoshone."

"You can't tell us apart, can you, Gunsmith? Most people can't. Stillox thinks he can, but I am sayin' he *thinks* he can!"

Clint said nothing, and now he felt the twin's horse moving closer. He realized what the man was up to. Had Stillox ordered it, or was it his own idea? Or maybe the two brothers had decided to brace him. Damn. He had enough to deal with in handling the wagons without this kind of thing. But he knew— and had known since he'd first laid eyes on those two—that it had to come. At the same time, he wondered where the other twin was. Under cover somewhere, backing his brother's play?

Suddenly the Gunsmith drew rein and turned Duke, almost hitting the man and horse beside him.

"We're heading back to the wagons," he said.

And before the surprise could leave the twin's face, he had kicked Duke into a gallop and was bearing down on the line of wagons. It was unfortunate, for he didn't like racing an animal in this kind of heat, but at the same time, he knew he had to catch the twins off guard—provided both of them were involved. And even if it were only the one man trying to keep up with Duke's fast pace now, then that had to be handled. Things such as this, the Gunsmith knew, had to be handled the minute they came up: right now.

In moments they were back at the wagon train and Clint had called a halt. The first person he saw up close was Stillox, seated on the front seat of the lead wagon, holding the lines of his mules. The second he saw was the other twin, riding a big steel-dust gelding at the far side of the wagon.

As he drew rein and waited for the twin to come up on his sorrel horse, he called out to Stillox.

"Pull up, Stillox. I want to talk with you and your two boys here." And he signaled the other twin to come up. Meanwhile all the wagons were pulling to a stop, their drivers calling out "Whoa!" and "Pull up there!"

Stillox stayed on his seat and wrapped his lines around the brake pole.

"What's goin' on, Adams? It ain't Injuns, I take it."

"I want something straightened out here with your two friends. And I want you and them to know it—that is, as long as you want me to guide your wagon train."

There was a grin on Stillox's face and he rubbed his chin hard, almost as though it itched. "Go ahead. You boys," he said, turning toward the twins, "you hear him out."

Clint turned to the twin who had ridden out to the point. "When I want to talk to either you or your brother, I will let you know. Meanwhile, you keep in your place, on account of I don't have time to listen to any more of that bullshit you were trying to hand me out yonder."

The twins said nothing. They sat their horses, as Clint also sat Duke, and looked at him.

"He wants a showdown," one of the twins said then: the one who had ridden out on the sorrel.

"Nole!" Stillox's voice was hard with authority. "Drop it!"

"Man's looking for trouble. It's clear as the nose

on his ass," Nole said, and his hand moved toward the bulge in his coat.

"Nole!"

But the Gunsmith had already moved. His hand had not gone for his gun but for the coiled lariat hanging from the pommel of his saddle, which he'd been unfastening while Nole was speaking, while at the same time moving Duke closer to the sorrel.

And now, in one blinding movement, he had seized the coiled rope and smashed it into the face of Nole. The twin's surprise was total, and he cried out in pain. The Gunsmith smashed him again with the hard coiled lariat. Then, unrolling the end with the leather thong sewn to it for cutting at cattle, he snapped it right into the big man's face; lengthening it, he snapped it like a whip at the hand of Clancy, who had begun reaching for his gun.

"That will be enough! Nole! Clancy!" roared the Reverend Stillox, now standing in the well of his Conestoga wagon with a Spencer .50-caliber repeating rifle in his hands.

The shock of the tremendous silence that fell on this dramatic tableau now ran through the entire wagon train.

"I am sorry about this, Adams," Stillox said, lowering the Spencer. "I apologize. My two hound dogs seem to have gotten carried away. And I must thank you for bringing them into line." He spat reflectively and without aim. "I sure admire the way you handle that rope. Surprised—though I reckon my two hound dogs are lucky—that you didn't handle your gun."

Clint had his eyes on the Twin Buttes as he said, "I only handle my gun when I shoot to kill. I think you boys better remember that. Huh, Clancy? Huh,

Nole!" And he looked at each one in turn, calling each by his right name.

"You can tell 'em apart!" Stillox said, and there was the fleck of admiration in his voice.

"Easy enough once I figured it out," Clint said, grinning. "But don't get the notion there's no hard feelings, boys," he said pleasantly. "Just behave yourselves, and we'll get along fine."

He turned toward Stillox now, aware of the people watching from their wagons. Some had climbed down and were standing there with their mouths open. He was looking for Molly, but he couldn't see her.

He turned his horse and touched his finger to the brim of his hat. "I'll be getting back to my work now, Stillox."

The twins had already ridden off toward the rear of the wagon train, and Stillox said, "If you're as fast with your gun as you are with that lariat, then those boys better behave it. Listen, tell me how you figure who is which."

"It's easy," Clint said soberly.

"Tell me how. I have a helluva time with figurin' it."

"Simple. One of them is all muscle and no brains. And the other has no brains and is all muscle." And with a friendly nod, he kicked his big black horse into a brisk canter.

But as he rode off he was thinking how that Spencer .50-caliber rifle in Stillox's hands had not been in the inventory offered when he'd ordered that all the weapons be shown to him.

* * *

He hadn't seen her, but he had thought of her; and he was thinking of her just now as he lay in his bedroll looking up at the thick gathering of stars that covered the night sky like a robe.

Then he heard—almost felt, really—the swish of a branch. And he was on his feet with the Colt in his fist. Listening. Keening toward the sound that had come so swifty, yet letting his listening widen, too, so that it was not narrowed onto one thing, for that could be fatal.

At length he knew it was her, even before he heard her softly calling, "Mr. Adams?"

Still, he didn't answer. It was always possible that she was being watched or had been forced into coming so that he would be caught off guard. Nobody, the Gunsmith well knew, reached old age on the Western frontier by being stupid.

Then she was there. She had entered the small clearing at the edge of which he had thrown his bedroll. She was nervous, he could tell right away, looking about as she came slowly across the little space that was grass.

"I'm here," he said. And then he said, "Molly..."

In the next moment she was in his arms and sobbing.

"Come, sit down. Over here. Tell me about it. I mean, if you want to."

He drew her down onto his bedroll, put his arm around her, and let her cry.

"I'm sorry. Oh, I am sorry. Such a fool." And she tried to stop, tried to hold her tears, and she dabbed at her eyes with a bandanna she was carrying. But she couldn't stop.

"Is something especially the matter, or is it just general?" he asked gently.

She was unable to speak. She only shook her head as it lay buried in his shoulder, and he continued to hold her.

"Let it all out," he said. "Let it go. You've been holding it in for too long."

"I'm sorry..."

"Stop that foolish talk. Just let it go."

And they sat like that for a good while, as he held her and she sobbed, almost stopped, and then started up again.

Finally she did stop, and he let her lie down on the bedroll. He lay quietly beside her. He was looking up at the stars and listening to the night sounds.

At last she said in her normal voice, "Thank you. Thank you for helping me.

He said nothing. He was content to lie there quietly, feeling her, smelling her; and wanting her in that quiet way.

Overhead the stars seemed even thicker, and he could tell by the slight sound and movement of her breathing that she was asleep.

He let her sleep, listening to the night sounds for any danger and thus far hearing none. After about an hour, he awakened her quietly.

"I fell asleep."

"I know. You'd better go back to your wagon now. They'll be wondering if something might have happened to you."

There was a little pause, and she said softly, "Something did."

He walked her a little way, and they stood within the protection of the trees, looking at the wagons.

"I am sorry I disturbed you," she said.

"I am not."

"May I come again?"

He slipped his arms around her then, and their lips met and they kissed.

When they drew back a little, though without dropping their arms, she said, "I am glad I came."

"I want you."

"I know."

"But we'll wait for the right time."

"I know."

He looked down into her face. "You be very careful. Especially now."

"I will be."

"They're watching everybody."

"I'll be careful."

And she was gone. He watched after her and listened, and then he went back to his bedroll and lay down and was almost immediately asleep—though, as always on the trail, just below the surface.

At around noon, Clint Adams ordered a halt.

"We'll water and rest them," he announced to the drivers. "Pull up close to the creek and check your axles, wheels, and, of course, your animals for sores and their harness. Any trouble, you tell me right now. Don't forget your weapons and ammo!"

"How far to Willow Crossing? When do you reckon we'll make it there?" Oleander Hildebrand was baldheaded, but he made up for it with a copious crop of chin whiskers, plus a great mustache.

"Tomorrow. We'll be in some time tomorrow, provided everything goes the way we hope." It was Hildebrand, driving the last wagon in the train, who was taking care of his gunsmithing wagon and bay team. Clint was pleased that the man was doing a good job.

Now, as he rode over to Hildebrand's wagon to take a look at the bays, he remembered how he'd heard quite by chance that Oleander was, or had been, the champion pie eater of Upper Sandusky, Indiana.

To his surprise and pleasure, he saw Molly Durham climbing down from the Hildebrand wagon.

"Hello," he said, admiring her body as she gracefully maneuvered the spokes of the big wagon wheel and dropped lightly to the ground, her cheeks flushed, her brown hair lying loosely on her head and around her shoulders. He thought she looked lovely, and he had to restrain himself from saying so.

"Life is always a surprise," he said, smiling at her.

"Indeed, sir? How so?" She was shining, without the slightest trace of her sorrow of the night before. She radiated health and an earthy sensuality that instantly found response between his legs.

"How so? Well, see, I came back here to see to my wagon and team of horses, and who do I run into? A beautiful young woman."

She flushed delightfully, and he felt his erection driving right through his trousers into the pommel of his stock saddle.

"Mr. Hildebrand asked me to keep an eye on them whenever he wasn't around, which I have been doing. I hope that was all right."

Clint turned toward the team. "This one here is Bud and this is Pete," he said, nodding to indicate which was which. "And they say they wouldn't trade you for a wagon full of oats. I can't argue with that, ma'am."

Her laughter tinkled in the hot almost breathless air.

"We'll water them," he said. "You want to give me a hand?"

"Sure do," she said with a slow, heavy accent.

And he cut his eye at her quickly to see if she were funning him by talking "Western"; but if she were, she had it well covered. She was watching him slip the bridle off Pete and draw on a hackamore. Seeing how intent she was, he said, "You try it. Get the hang of it." And he waited while she slipped off Bud's bridle and pulled on the halter he handed her.

"Good enough," he said. "I see you know your way around horses some."

"I had a good teacher," she said.

"Yeah? Who?"

"Young man named Clint Adams."

They laughed together at that as they led the bays down to the creek.

Later, walking back and leading the horses, he said, "You know how to hobble a horse?"

"I'd like to learn how."

He reached into his wagon and took out a set of rawhide hobbles.

"See, Duke there, he's been broke to groundhitching, but these two never were. That's why we have to hobble them. Though by now I don't think they'd run off. Excepting if there was trouble, like gunfire, something like that, they could spook and take off. See?"

"Gotcha!"

And once again he checked fast to see if she were

teasing. He knew, of course, that she was, and it pleased him; yet he played his role in the game with a stern look and a "shrewd" glance at her. All the time, he wanted to lead her into the bushes. But, again, the moment was not "appropriate."

He showed her how to put on the hobbles, then told her to do so on the second bay. It pleased him greatly to see how handy she was.

"Can I look at some of your gunsmith stuff?" she asked when they had finished with the horses. "Or am I being nosey?"

"What do you want to know?"

"I don't know. Maybe everything. But, specifically, about guns I feel I need to know something. I mean, if I'm going to be living in the Wild West, as they call it back home."

He had pulled back the heavy tarp that covered his tools and equipment, and she sat on the edge of the wagon box and looked down in fascination at the array of guns and parts of guns; though many of them were wrapped and tied with pigging string, there were some parts that were not, plus two complete weapons minus their cylinders.

"I take it that none of these can work the way they are, so it's all right to leave them in the wagon like this," she said.

"That's right. They're not a bit of good to anybody who hasn't got the missing parts, plus the time and know-how to assemble them. And, plus—how to shoot."

"I have heard that mostly you point and pull. Though I do suspect there's something more to it than just that."

WAGON TRAIN TO HELL 59

"I think there's more to riding a bucking horse than just holding onto that saddlehorn."

"Sure. Sure," she said.

She was sure bright and she was sure goodlooking. And he was sure horny as all hell for her.

But she was saying something now. About the rifle she'd seen someone carrying that was different from the other guns the men had.

"Who?" he asked.

"Mr. Stillox. It looked brand new, at least to me, who knows nothing about guns."

"I'd say you know a good half of it, ma'am."

"How's that?" She squinted at him, the sun in her eyes, and rubbed the palms of her hands together in front of her.

"Like you know how to see things. That's the most important. With anything. With guns, with horses, with this here country. With people." He began to point out guns to her.

"Huh," she said, and her nose twitched. "Huh," she said again. Then: "Yes, I believe that is so. That's right."

"That gun there," he said, "is the same as the one Stillox has, though broken down, as you can see. It's a Spencer .50 caliber, adapted to the Spencer special .56-.52 rimfire cartridge. It's just like the one Spencer himself used at the official tests that won him his contract." He stopped and looked around to see whether anyone was within listening distance before continuing: "There's also the Spencer carbine using a .56-.50 cartridge, amongst others, and the army used them. Custer had 'em at the Washita when he wiped out the Indians but didn't have them at the Little Big Horn, when the Indians wiped out him and his men. Right now, not only the army of the West but each and every man-jack around would give plenty to lay his hands on one of those Spencers."

She said nothing but just stood there looking into the middle distance, as though thinking of what he had just told her and maybe where to place it.

"Have you seen any other Spencers about—I mean, in the wagon train?"

"I don't think so. Do you want me to take a look?"

"Just notice if you can, without anyone getting excited. I need to know."

"Sure," she said. And then again: "Sure."

He squinted into the sky.

"Time to move out?" she asked.

He nodded. "What'll you do when we get to Willow Crossing? Stay with the wagons?"

"I don't know. It depends if I locate the man I'm looking for. Someone back where we started gave me to understand that the man either was—or might be—in this wagon train. Like I said, I want to find him."

"And then what?"

"Bring him to justice."

"That might be a good bit harder than finding him."

"I know. I guess I know that."

"Be careful," Clint said then. "Be careful he doesn't find you."

"I will, I will. Thank you."

Clint wanted to say more, but at that moment he saw Hildebrand walking toward them, so he touched the brim of his hat to the girl and turned toward the knobby, grizzled man who at certain moments struck him as simply an old stove-up bronc buster and at other times almost like a man who might have a pretty fair notion of who he was.

At the Double Bar Cross, L. T. Moses, the ranch foreman, was sitting on the top rail of the round horse corral, watching two of his men sack a wild buckskin yearling. The two men—along with L. T., when the spirit moved him—had been working over three of the new mustangs that had been recently run in. The particular horse in question, a gelding, was giving those hands all they could handle. He had one rear leg tied up, so he was actually three legged, pulling against the halter rope that held him to the corral post, while the men—Buck Stinson and Stringer Jack Giddens—slapped him with old sacking to get him used to movement around his head and body. Nobody had tried saddling the bucksin yet; nobody—at least not Stinson and Stringer Jack—was in any hurry to try topping him. He was tough, like most buckskins, and as L. T. Moses had cautioned his boys, "He ain't a hoss to mess with, less you want a fast ticket to hell."

L. T., a man famous for his sour disposition and acid, pan-faced humor, took out a wooden Lucifer and his trail knife and fashioned himself a neat toothpick. Then, working the toothpick around his mouth, he took a sack of Bull Durham and some papers out of his shirt pocket and began building himself a smoke. He rolled it real neat, not spilling any, licked it, twisted the end, gave another lick the whole length of the cigarette, and stuck the end on his lower lip. The toothpick was in the other corner of his mouth as he struck a Lucifer one handed on his thumbnail and lit up, canting his head just right toward the flame. All without taking his eyes off the men who were sacking the tough little bronc.

"He looks like a good one," Buck Stinson said, as at a signal from their foreman they stopped the sacking. "He gets to handle that sack he can handle a rope or damn near anything flying around his head."

Stringer Jack spat into a pile of fresh horse manure and scratched into his left armpit. "Goddam whores is gettin' too damn easy about the company they keep," he said with a grin.

"Just so's you don't start pissin' razor blades," L. T. said. 'You boys be careful. I need every damn man I got."

L.T. swung down from the corral and now stood in front of the two men. "Want you to get the hands together—exceptin' the outriders of course, Pinky and Dutch—but everybody else. McTeague's coming out."

"When d'you want the men?" Stinson asked. "Right now?"

L.T. squinted at the sky. "I'd say around the middle of the forenoon like. But keep alert to it. You know how he is. Sometimes he pops right up on you when you don't know how the hell he got there."

As he spoke he squinted his left eye, canting his head in the direction of the trail leading down from the ranch houses near the top of the high lip of land, which gave anyone at the Double Bar Cross a long view of an approaching rider.

"You mean, like right now!" boomed a voice from the corner of the bunkhouse, which was directly behind them.

"Shit," muttered L. T. And he stripped his smoke,

WAGON TRAIN TO HELL   63

turning to see Riot McTeague coming toward them with a cold smile on his big red face. "Good thing I am a friendly, wouldn't you say!"

"You don't sound so friendly to me," L.T. said. "But then, by God, what if I tolt you we had you covered from the shithouse yonder!" He jerked his thumb in the direction of the lone outhouse and called out, "Hey, Jeremy, leave your Sharps inside and come on out and meet Mr. McTeague."

"Jesus!" muttered McTeague, not quite believing this latest humor of his ranch foreman—but putting up with it nonetheless. "Pretty damn clever, L. T. Now you know for a damn fact why I hired you as ramrod." He paused, looking closely at the outhouse as a thin figure stepped into view. "Exceptin' I don't see no Sharps."

"I told him to leave it inside!" L. T., a veteran of the range as well as the world of repartee, came back swift as a snake.

"Tell him to get it," McTeague said, in a good humor and so going along with his sometimes dicey foreman. "Tell him I want to see that piece."

"I'd say maybe it fell down the hole," L. T. said as the young man, Jeremy, raised his hands, shrugging to say that he couldn't produce the Sharps.

"Moses," said McTeague, his mood suddenly changing. "You quit that funning now. Just mind, I got a use for you and that this is no time for anything else."

"That is what I know. But you caught me out and I had to think of something fast. Wasn't good enough, that's all. But a man's got to keep trying."

But McTeague had had enough by now, and his face said so. "You're too smart for your own good,

Moses. Maybe that name you got fooled you all this time. But it don't fool me. Just remember that there is certain situations a man can't get out of, no matter how many dumb jokes he tries. Like, for instance, gettin' out of a pine box."

An appalling silence suddenly fell on the three men and the boy, Jeremy. Buck Stinson and Stringer Jack Giddens were both mighty glad that they weren't L. T. Moses; L. T. was damn sorry he was.

Still, the gingery moment passed. L. T., after all, was just about the best ramrod in that part of the country, and everybody, including himself as well as Riot McTeague, knew it. McTeague needed L. T. But L. T. was aware of his weakness for funning at inappropriate moments, and while knowing how he had to be careful as hell with a man like McTeague, he still couldn't always check himself quickly enough. Like just now. At the same time, L. T., like a number of men who'd seen it all, and could have told it all but didn't, still didn't believe in letting another man top him—even if he was handing him his pay every month.

McTeague, for his part, didn't mind his foreman horsing around near as much as he let on. He knew the other man wasn't trying to put him down; there wasn't a man alive who could. So he stuck with his motto: Get all the juice you can out of a man, but don't squeeze him dry; remember that when you let him come back you can use him again. Except, of course, those who stepped too far. Those fools were rare—or had been, before they began to take up part of the landscape. L. T. Moses had his uses, and so long as he had his uses he could keep his juices— according to the little jingle that Riot McTeague sometimes enjoyed telling to himself and sometimes even to others.

He stood now in the big window of the big ranch house he had built. It was a handsome house built of straight, true spruce, which had been felled up on the mountain, limbed and snaked down the hard, snow-packed trail behind the big bay horse, then stacked on the drying rack and peeled with a draw knife and left to cure. Then in the spring, he had built the first cabin, now the main room, using only a short-handled axe for coping each log's end so that it would fit snug over the corner log to make a right angle. The chinking came next, and then the whole shebang was rubbed with linseed oil—logs and chinking and the pine flooring brought over from Ting Lapham's sawmill down at Catlin. The roof was rough lumber. Fancy, not like the barn, which had a sod roof, flat with grass grown on it like hair, and unpeeled logs. Later he added a room at a time as needed.

McTeague was a man who did things himself but not in older years, for while still more than able, he was too busy to engage in that kind of physical work. He had men to do it.

And he had built much of Willow Crossing. When he'd first come there, the town was a wreck, a ghost town of crumbling log cabins, washed-out soddies, and with a population of not even a hundred souls. The town had been wiped out by Indians, bandits, and Civil War border gangs—whether from the North or the South made no difference. Each time the town of Willow Crossing disappeared, only for some strange reason to appear again. Probably because it was in the way of the herds coming north and so was needed.

But Riot McTeague had seen beyond the wretched hovels; he had seen a real town. And he had worked to make it so. It was his town. Then he had moved out and built his ranch.

He was a man who knew something about himself. He knew he couldn't just set. It wasn't in his nature. He had to be building, moving, reaching out. And after a while, he began to see his new plan. His biggest plan yet. He saw it as he looked at the prairies and the mountains. But he needed men. Not just men such as Moses, who could do their job and do it well; but men with imagination, brains, daring, but also men who knew how to follow orders, men who could be deputized and relied on.

Right now he needed someone to work the town for him while he made his big push out by Stud Basin, that section of land as big as some Eastern states.

He knew the man he wanted. And he'd sent for him. He had been mighty gratified to hear that Fancy Joe Stillox was on his way. And when he'd heard too that some gunfighter with a reputation had joined up with Joe's wagon train, well, that was all right. Fancy Joe could handle that. He had known Joe from way back, way back in the New Orleans days. He didn't trust him, but that wasn't important. What was important was that he knew how to use him.

But there was one thing he didn't like. And he said so to his foreman as he stood in the big window of his big room and looked out over his land, running as far as he could see.

WAGON TRAIN TO HELL 67

"I don't like what I hear about this English tenderfoot coming out here from Boston or London or some God damn fancypants place and thinking he's going to hunt all over the place like that duke or whatever the hell he was from Russia. The one that come out with Custer."

"That wasn't around here," L. T. said, eyeing the bottle of whiskey; and so, minus his full attention for the subject raised by McTeague, he stuck his foot in it.

"That's what I know, for Christ sake!" snapped McTeague, spinning around quickly from the window. "Listen, will you! I said, *like* that fancy-ass duke. But he—this new one—he is figuring to hunt around *here*."

"But it's your range, so we can keep him off," said L. T., trying to recover lost ground.

"Exceptin' it ain't mine. Not yet. It is government land. Shit, you're a cattleman and you don't know that! Jesus!"

"Forgot," said L. T.

"Just don't forget your ass, dammit, when you walk over there to get that bottle and hand it to me!" snapped McTeague.

He remained with his back to the window, feeling the lowering sun on his shoulders, his kidneys. It was good. He just wished he could find a foreman with some brains. Moses was good with the men; no problem there. He was good with the stock. He knew horses, cattle, everything you had to know about feed, cattle driving; he was a top hand. But somehow, for anything else, for a long sight on something, the man was as dumb as a bell with no clapper.

"I want to talk to you about this lord or whatever the hell he claims to be. We have got to do some good thinking on it."

"What about his having like an accident?" L. T. said. "It can happen."

"I have already thought of that. But I'd better tell you something about this lord. I am told that he is no fool. Also, he is well known and has rich and powerful friends in Washington. You get the picture?"

"I do." L. T. held up his glass of whiskey and studied its color as the sunlight came pouring through the window.

"Are you listening to me?"

L. T. sat up in his chair. "Yes, I am. But I still say maybe something like an accident..." He didn't finish the sentence, letting McTeague fill it for himself.

McTeague came closer now and sat down. He leaned forward, holding his ranch foreman with his hard eyes. "I want one thing understood and understood good, Moses. By the men, and especially by yourself."

"Huh?" The foreman sat forward now, hearing something special in his boss's voice.

"I want no one—NO ONE—to bugger this man. You do nothing without I tell you."

L. T.'s mouth dropped open, and his eyes bugged. "Boss, don't I always?"

"You're damn right you do. And right now I want you to be God damn sure you remember that!"

There was a knock at the door.

"Come!" McTeague called the word out hard.

The door opened and a cowhand appeared, with his hat off, as per instructions from way back.

"There's two men, Mr. McTeague. Two men come. They look like buff hunters. One says to tell you Mick Folio, I believe he said."

"Two, you said."

"The other was with him. He didn't say his name."

"Tell them to wait. And you wait outside."

The cowboy—he was a young man—nodded and closed the door carefully behind him.

"Buff hunters?" L. T. Moses put his glass down on the table and stood up. "Buff hunters in this country? Hell, the buffalo bin hunted out since—"

McTeague cut him off. "They're wolfers."

"Wolfers!" The foreman canted his head and squinted at his boss. "They got anything to do with that lord feller wanting to hunt? I mean, don't that English dude know there's about enough buffalo meat around here to physic a jaybird?"

"He's a big-game hunter. But maybe not buffalo."

"What then?"

Riot McTeague stood for a quiet moment in front of his foreman. "Has it by now figgered in you, Mr. Moses, that maybe that dumb English lord might really be after something else?" And then he added in disgust, "Fer Christ sake!"

McTeague walked to the window. And with his back to the room and his foreman standing in the middle of it with the surprise not yet wiped off his face, he said, "Send them two in—on your way out."

L. T. did as he was told, and as he rode out to take

a look at the little buckskin bronc, he was remembering as clearly as though it were right in front of him —and right now—the time down at Miller's Tunnel Saloon, just outside in the back, when Riot McTeague at fifty feet holed three silver dollars with three shots after they'd been stuck on Miller's back fence.

FIVE

"I still hold that feller can't be trusted." It was Clancy Hooligan speaking to his twin brother, Nole, and to the Reverend Stillox, who was trimming his fingernails with a Bowie knife.

"Nobody's askin' you to trust him. I told you both that when I hired him on as scout and wagon master."

"Don't know why you hired the son-of-a-bitch," Nole said.

"So's we could get where we were heading for—Willow Crossing."

They were seated inside the Stillox wagon and Dolores, a young widow traveling with her brother and his two children, had just served them supper, Amelia being "under the weather."

"You said you didn't trust him," Clancy said.

"That's the main reason I hired him: so's I could

keep an eye on him. I still think he suspicioned somethin' about the Spencers." The reverend sucked his teeth vigorously.

"But he didn't even see them," Clancy said. And he looked at his twin, who verified the statement by nodding his big bullet head.

"That Adams is a shrewd one," Stillox said. "He like reads a man's mind now and again, like. Still, we will outsmart him. Never fear. Fancy Joe is smarter," he said, muttering now as though in a reverie.

The twins looked at him and then at each other dully.

"The Sioux have them weapons now, according to the agreement worked out by McTeague," Stillox said. "But they have got no ammo. So they won't be no use to them." He still spoke as though addressing no one in particular, yet his voice was strong. "As per instructions," he went on, "and as per that smartass Injun Raven knows. He has got to get ammo somewheres else." He looked at the twins, smiling gold at them. "Why they haven't attacked us?" He chuckled. "My idea, that: keepin' the weapons and the ammo separate until we was safely where we was going." He watched them carefully, making sure they believed his story.

He stood up, but his head was touching the canvas side of the wagon top where it dipped. "We ought to be there by tomorrow," he said heavily and sniffed.

"Where?" asked Clancy with a puzzled look on his face.

"Willow Crossing. Where'n hell you think, for Christ sake!"

"Dumbbell," said Nole sourly.

"Go fuck yerself," Clancy said, the color rising into his thick face.

"Easy, gentlemen. Easy," cautioned Stillox, looking a bit nervously toward the opening of the canvas-topped wagon. "You never know who might have big ears. Let's keep our business private."

The twins glared at each other but said nothing further. With an inaudible sigh of relief, the Reverend Joseph Stillox ducked through the opening of the wagon and climbed down to the ground.

For a moment he stood where he was, blinking his eyes. It was evening, and the members of the wagon train were cleaning up after their evening meal, which they had had together.

"Our last night," Stillox said solemnly as an elderly man and his wife walked past him. "We'll be in Willow Crossing tomorrow forenoon, Adams tells me."

"Good, Reverend. Very good. And God bless you." Smiling sanctimoniously, Stillox nodded, and at the same time he wondered where Clint Adams was. And he wondered, too, how much the man known as the Gunsmith might suspect about the transfer of Spencer rifles to the Sioux under cover of an Indian attack.

He was also wondering how much longer he could handle the twins, who were growing more rambunctious each day. Well, they had their uses: Mostly they frightened people just by the way they looked, the way they were. And they were loyal; he had to remember that. They always did anything and everything he wanted. Not a bad thing to have on your side, he reflected. And that thought allowed him to expand and even feel glad he had those two stalwarts at his side.

Presently, as he took a short stroll around the camp before turning in, his thoughts began to consider the coming rendezvous in Willow Crossing. He hadn't seen Riot McTeague in quite a spell; and he thought it was going to be a good meeting. He was sure it would be. They had both gone to a whole lot of trouble to work things out. And Fancy Joe was grateful. Grateful for the action. For what was life without the action?

Under the soft velvet night sky, the two bodies were intertwined, their passion seething through them, spilling into the wild air around them as a gust of wind swept across the meadow, warming and cooling at the same time. The lovers, having consummated their passion, now rested.

"I am so happy." Molly was almost whispering her words.

"You need to be," Clint said. Turning toward her, he lifted his body slightly and looked at her naked breasts under the light of the clear full moon.

He had not intended to have her when she appeared just after he'd reached his bedding, having resigned himself to waiting at least until they'd reached Willow Crossing. But it had simply happened. One moment she was standing in front of him, and then—that fabulous gesture pushing her soft brown hair back from her ears—and it was all over but the shouting, as he told himself. The next thing they were both naked and he was on top of her, mounting her eagerly, passionately, with his erection like a fence post. Yet he moved slowly, gently—wanting it that way, knowing that way was the best. Only he did not decide so, did not think it, but followed both their instincts. For both bodies knew what was needed. Thought had no place here. Indeed, there was room for nothing but desire, passion, an unbelievable force—the strongest thing he knew and, at the same time, the gentlest. And he saw now that the stronger, the more powerful his desire, the gentler his approach to her.

And she was the same. He could feel her burning as he cupped his hand over one of her perfectly shaped breasts and played with its rigid nipple, until both of them thought they would go mad.

Leaning down, he sucked and teased the thick nipple with his tongue, his teeth. Then, raising himself up as she reached to his penis and drew him closer, he reached back to slip his fingers in her bush, fingering the slippery slit, with its lips extended now. She guided his great organ to her breast and rubbed the wet slit of his erection onto her nipple. The next thing he knew, she had him deep down her throat and was sucking deliriously, with exquisite slowness, while her lively tongue tickled and licked the whole length of his shaft. Finally she tried to get his balls in her mouth, but they were too big. Yet she did manage one and sucked it joyously while she fisted his glistening organ.

He could endure it no longer, turning on her now so that he could kiss her bush, her vagina, while she again sucked him slowly and completely.

When they came up for air, they were both gasping. But without the least hesitation they righted their position, so that he was on top of her, facing her, while she lifted her legs high and he rode her, his hands supporting her deliciously pumping buttocks, their mouths pressed together, allowing the minimum of air necessary. And now, finding their finest stroke in the identical rhythm of the two bodies that were one, neither could bear it any longer and at last both came in great squirts, their bodies taking over completely, with no thought, no direction or intention. Both of them were willing slaves to the dancing of their exquisite joy. Then came the bliss of the melting of their spent bodies, their selves, and they lay side by side, holding hands, and they slept.

Later, it was as though they had both been awakened at the very same second.

"Mr. Adams..."

"Mrs. Durham..."

Her laughter tinkled in the air.

"Clint..."

"Is Molly for Margaret?" he asked.

"Molly is for Molly."

He turned over onto his stomach, lifting himself up so that he could look down at her. "I see you're one of those people, and I'm glad."

"One of what people?" And her voice was filled with teasing, which delighted him.

"The kind that rides their own trail and doesn't let anyone get in front of them."

"I like that. You are that way. I reckon," she added, and he again caught the teasing in her voice.

"I reckon I am," he said. "A man's got to sail his own boat is how I look at it."

"And a woman."

"I guess you just have to take me like you find me," he said, teasing her in return.

"Any time, sir. Any time at all."

"Wolfers," L. T. Moses was saying. "Don't figure what you want with wolfers. Course it's your bizness...."

Riot McTeague scratched deep into his thick black beard, staring out of his baby-blue eyes at his ranch foreman, and he chuckled. He chuckled deep in his throat, the kind of chuckle that often accompanied a salacious remark; confiding, knowledgeable with special meaning, and low-down dirty.

"They're so God damn dirty," L. T. went on. "They stink. Them two you saw—I smelt 'em all the way back down to the barn. I mean—Jesus on a raft!"

McTeague's eyes danced with merriment. He loved to shock people, especially people like L. T., who were usually totally unshockable, people who could accept anything from a broken arm to a slashed gut to a buckshot-riddled body dying in agony. To shock such a person was good sport!

"Why I want 'em? Listen, I'm figuring maybe on more of those mavericks coming in."

"Holy Mother of God!" The words sprang unbidden from the tough ramrod's lips. To his own astonishment, for they reminded him of his mother, upon whose lips those words were frequent in her usually successful battles with the world. He was sure she had uttered them on her deathbed, though he had not been present.

"So you're gonna stink everybody to death, whatever your plan is," said L. T. drily. "Maybe that's as good a way as any. And it saves gunpowder, for sure." He canted his head at his employer. "What they gonna do here? You can't hide 'em. Not that stink! And nobody's gonna believe they're here chasing wolves, since there ain't a wolf between here an' Texas."

"That's right, there is not," said McTeague, careful with his English as, in fact, he sometimes was. This was a fact noted by a number of people in the Territory, and it was assumed that Riot McTeague had been well educated and had perhaps even attended college. But of course no one ever asked him.

"Then why?" L. T. insisted. "If they be working here at the Double Bar, I got to know something about 'em."

McTeague grinned. "Well, you know wolfers, I can tell. You have got the right attitude toward same. Give a wolfer a wide piece of room." He sniffed. "Like you say, people don't like the breed, number one. Number two, a wolfer is mean enough to do anything. Course for money."

"Well, I know they used to pull in a good lot of money in the old days when the buffs were around and the hunters left the carcasses all over the prairie, and the wolves were thicker'n fleas on a dog's balls."

McTeague was nodding. "I put in a piece of time myself with some of them when I was a buff hunter. Along with doing some skinning. I'll say the only thing dirtier and meaner than a skinner—and more ornery—is a wolfer. I mind how some of those men used to bring in three, four thousand come spring. Some even more. Shit, all you needed was a gutted buff carcass, with strychnine mixed in with the blood and entrails, and by God that'd take care of fifty wolves. Maybe more!"

"A right profitable business," L. T. agreed.

"Now it's mostly up in Montana," McTeague said reflectively. "Wolf around this part of the country used to average about a hundred pounds. That is a whole helluva lot of angry animal, let me tell you! He'd stand maybe thirty, thirty-two inches at the shoulder."

"That is what I know," L. T. said sagely. Like Riot McTeague, L. T. Moses savored the old days, though not to the detriment of his own survival in the present. McTeague knew this about his foreman. One reason why he kept him. They didn't make men like L. T. anymore. Nor himself, and that was for sure by God.

"It's for sure the damn wolfers are pretty close to the wolves, ain't it," L. T. said. "And I can see why you want 'em. You wantin' me to ramrod them?"

"I never have given a man a job to do I can't do myself," McTeague said.

"I know that." L. T. sighed, accepting the decision. "They'll do what I tell them," he said. "You just need to let me know what you want."

McTeague was looking out the window, with his back to his foreman now. "I will handle them," he said. "Good for a man to keep his hand in, wouldn't you say?"

The foreman of the Double Bar Cross stared at the big man's back, hearing something he didn't quite get in those words. But he did catch the opening and closing, the flexing of McTeague's hands.

The foreman of the Double Bar Cross felt something different, something foreign in the atmosphere of the room then. It was there only for a flash. Then it was gone.

And yes, L. T. Moses understood. Riot McTeague was maybe feeling his years.

More often than not, the more lively Western towns kept a division, or "deadline," separating the respectable part from that other area often referred to as "Crib City." Frequently it was the railroad tracks that marked the separation. Even so, there was an inevitable exchange between the two. In other words, as the Reverend Joseph Stillox—otherwise known as Fancy Joe—put it, the difference between Heaven and Hell wasn't all that clear. And, as the reverend also put it, "A man can take his pick!" But there was never any question in anyone's mind that those gents from the right side who had never ventured into the excitements and pleasures of Crib City were rare as snowballs in Hell.

Here, of course, those colorful individuals—the gamblers, con men and bunco artists, transient cowboys, miners, prospectors, and hunters, not to mention the ubiquitous drummers who were infiltrating the West more and more, as well as those individuals with summer names and unquestioned pasts—cavorted round the clock with booze, music, song and dance, with cards, dice, and assuredly with those lively individuals to whom the more pious, straitlaced, and righteous referred to as "cyprians," "soiled doves," or simply "fallen women."

Of course, the drinking establishments were on both sides of the deadline in many towns, the deadline usually being labeled—and only sometimes enforced—by a town marshal. For instance, cattle towns that suffered the periodic arrival of riotous Texans hot off the long dusty trail from below the Red River would be completely taken over by the highjinks of those cow waddies in the absence of at least a semblance of law and order.

In Willow Crossing there was no railroad, nor any deadline. The fact was, with the exception of a certain area beyond the outskirts of the town, the whole place was a Crib City or Cabbage Patch. The town consisted of a dozen or so roughly built frame houses, two dance halls, four straight saloons, a hotel called the Frisco House, a livery, a dry-goods store that also sold hardware and guns and ammo, and two eateries. It was a brown, dusty, and dull-looking town, like so many of its kind. Like something that had just appeared on the prairie—which indeed it had—and with a future that could only be termed questionable. Willow Crossing could have disappeared on any day in any year and would not have been mourned. A recent Easterner who happened to be passing through—nobody knew why—had described Willow Crossing as a place with no past, no future, and a most dubious present.

Yet there were certain evidences of change. At one edge of town two new buildings were going up. Plus there were rumors about further developments. All of this activity, which wasn't really stirring the populace into great enthusiasm, was credited to Riot McTeague. At the same time, and perhaps as a result of McTeague's enterprise, almost without anyone noticing, the separation between the citizens who lived by honest toil and those who lived otherwise had vanished, along with the distinction between "the other side of the tracks" and the rest of it. The Reverend Joseph Stillox, always an excruciatingly observant man, had commented in his usual pithy mode. "It is democracy at work," he deponed within only a few hours of his arrival in Willow Crossing. "All are equal in opportunity and the pursuit of happiness. And, of course, the Lord."

These felicitous words were uttered on a patch of ground on which the reverend conducted Sunday service, for it happened to be the Lord's day on which the wagon train had arrived. And, to be sure, the Reverend Stillox was adroit in pointing this out to his "congregation," which consisted of the members of the wagon train plus half a dozen hangers-on who happened to be there at the moment.

"Word has been brought to me of a man who is helping Willow Crossing to become more than just a sink of iniquity for the devilish pleasures of the immoral and debased," the reverend intoned. "I am speaking of a man I have never met but whose shining vision has reached even beyond Willow Crossing, showing the way toward building a strong and noble—a God-fearing—West! I refer, of course, to Mr. Riot McTeague."

He paused, his eyes rolling toward the sky, while the Gunsmith, listening at the edge of the small crowd, wondered if Stillox were going to overdo it.

"It is not beyond the realm of our search for happiness and good, clean honest lives to admire and— yes—*revere* a man who can point the way! A moment of silent prayer, then, for Mr. Riot McTeague, who is building! Building the West in this stark, dangerous, and backward frontier!"

Well, reflected Clint Adams as he stood there in a state of dumbfounded admiration for the little man standing bareheaded and with those Twin Buttes flanking him in the dazzling Sunday sunlight. Well at least he asked for a *silent* prayer.

"Jesus!" said a quiet voice at his elbow. "That jasper's got more balls than a man can shake a stick at!" The words were just above a whisper, but they were clear. And Clint saw that they came from Oleander Hildebrand, he who had helped him with his team and gunsmithing wagon. The knobby man was standing there firm as a branch on a cottonwood tree, his lined face wrapped in wonder at what he had just heard.

It was at that moment that Clint Adams's impression of the man came close to expression. In a word, he saw that he'd been quite right about him. Hildebrand was one of those rare types of person whom you realized that you already knew; a man who in a sense knew himself. And he could see that Oleander Hildebrand felt the same about the Gunsmith.

The game was stud with deuces wild. In the gaming room of the Inside Straight Saloon & Gaming Parlor & Dance Palace, the players sat attentively, hunched over their cards. They were earnest and serious as they ringed the round baize-topped table, while a small collection of hangers-on stood about, watching the play.

Among the watchers of the game was the Reverend Stillox, regarding each play carefully from under hooded eyes. From time to time he sighed, and between hands he even discoursed on the droll situation he had found himself in, spending time in a saloon and gambling parlor.

"Most interesting," he was saying now. "Most,

most interesting. A man of God spending time in a gambling establishment. Shocking? No, not so. Not in the light of our purpose. Our purpose, let me swiftly say, is to educate, lead those who are lost, and return them to the better path, the clear vision, the erect fortitude needed for a whole life."

At first these intermittent remarks were ignored by the players and others in the room who could hear him; and after a while there were those who sneered at the reverend's observations. And finally, after more time had passed—and always speaking between hands, never while the play was on—the reverend had become a part of the scene; he had achieved his purpose.

So now, as one of the players stood up to leave, he declared, "I've had a sudden thought: If as a man of God I must know the Devil's ways, I must gain true knowledge of how he operatees. And that can only be done by engaging in his actions. Gentlemen, I am going to pay the great sacrifice, provided you will allow me, and shall play a few hands. I believe I have the hang of it now."

Without waiting for an answer he opened his coat, drew back his hand, reached to his pocket, and pulled out a not-small stake with which he wished to play. The movement did not pass unnoticed by the players or those watching, and a stir ran through the group.

"Sit down, sir. Sit down," said the dealer.

"Thank you, sir," said Stillox, and then, looking across the table, he saw that Clint Adams was among the group watching the game. "Ah, Scout Adams, glad you're here. You might want to advise me, since I am new at this sort of thing. Oh, I did play cards of some kind many years ago, as a, uh, boy." His smiling, innocent face went round the assembled players, as though waiting for one of them to say yes or no to his suggestion of Clint helping him. But not even an eyelash flickered. It was as he wanted it; it was as he'd expected. And, too, it was good that Adams was there. It would make him sharper. And, having studied his plan, he knew he would have to be.

A new dealer took charge now and announced that the game would be jacks or better. He was a thin, angular man with a lot of hair in his nostrils. Expertly he shuffled, cut, and dealt. He leaned back slightly in his round-backed chair with his lips pursed, eyebrows lifted, and his lids lowered as he bent his attention to his cards.

The game proceeded without incident, and Stillox, playing the role of the innocent with relish, noted that Clint Adams wasn't missing a thing. Well, it was the acid test then. Adams would be there to verify. It couldn't have worked out better, he told himself, as he lost again.

"I'd like to try my hand at dealing," he said suddenly. "I mean, of course, if that goes with the rules of the game."

He did not see the smile that Clint Adams was having a great deal of difficulty in suppressing. Clint, meanwhile, had suddenly noticed that one of the men watching from across the table, in the second row and almost behind the new dealer, was Oleander Hildebrand. Interesting, Clint thought, that a man who looked like an old bronc stomper should be here. Who was he? He'd heard he was a champion pie eater from some town in Indiana, whatever that meant, and he had a good feeling about the man; but that was all.

But he had no time for these thoughts now. Stillox had shuffled and was now cutting the cards. Clint noticed that he had shortened the long nail on his little finger. The man was really sacrificing himself for the role.

Stillox had asked for a fresh deck of cards, and though Clint was watching him closely, he saw nothing out of line. The reverend dealt slowly, fumbling a little, making sure that everyone noticed he was somewhat out of his depth. He had lost a few pots and not won anything thus far. Clint could see that the players were at ease and had finally accepted this strange turn of events; one or two were even smiling indulgently. Interesting, he reflected, what greed will do to an otherwise sensible man.

"Ante a dollar," Stillox said. "If that's all right. Is it all right?" His questioning eyes swept the table.

Somebody grunted assent.

One of the players said, "Pass."

A man with a shiny bald head opened. "I'll make it a dollar for a starter."

"Looks like I'm in," the man next to him said, and he took a drink from the glass at his elbow. His hair was very red.

The reverend Stillox looked at his cards and said nothing. He seemed neither nervous nor fearful. And as far as the Gunsmith could tell, his companions very likely figured he was so innocent that fear had no place in him. Such a man—a preacher—clearly had to be a man without guile. You had to respect that; though it didn't mean you had to indulge such a lack of worldliness.

A man wearing a battered Stetson—obviously a cowhand—tossed in a silver cartwheel and said nothing.

After a good bit of hesitation, and after casting his eyes about, Stillox—a reverend to the marrow of his bones, Clint noted—announced that he would stay.

The man who at the beginning had passed pushed forward a dollar and drew two cards.

The red-headed man said, "I'll take three cards." He looked at the three cards Stillox dealt him and tossed them into the discard. Sniffing, he sat back in his chair, scratching behind his left ear.

The bald-headed man released a gentle belch as he examined his cards. "Well, hell . . . I oughta pass, but let's see where the men are and where the boys, eh?" He grinned suddenly.

"Let's see where your money is, Billy boy!" said the red-headed man. "Put it in the pot and never mind the smart talk!"

The bald-headed man looked across at Stillox, who was staring into his cards, almost as though he were lost. "All right then," he said. "Table stakes? All right? I'm betting five."

The man who had passed and then bet a dollar and drew two cards now pushed five dollars into the pot. "And another five," he said, counting it out in cartwheels.

"I pass," said the cowboy.

"And another five," said the bald-headed man.

"I call your five and raise you five more," said the man who had raised the man with the bald head.

The bald-headed man was holding his cards tightly in both hands, curving them. "I will see you and raise you five," he said.

At that point the Reverend Joseph Stillox said, "I call . . . Is that right to say—'I call'?"

"Sure is," said someone in the group of watchers, drawing furious looks from the men seated at the table.

"And I raise the pot another ten dollars," said the reverend.

Astonishment took over at the table. Mouths dropped open, and eyes widened, followed by pique flashing across various faces.

"Well, by God, and damnit to hell!" said the red-headed man, who was out of it. "I wonder if you got four of a kind there, Preacher."

"Only one way to find out," somebody muttered as gloom gripped the table.

"Everybody in?" the red-headed man asked. Having tossed in his hand, he was obviously enjoying the drama.

"I am," said the cowboy. "By damn, let's have a look-see." He leaned forward with his eyes on Stillox's hands, his mouth ajar, his eyes wide.

"Men, I'll be happy to pay for a round," said the reverend, as he put down four kings and an ace and pulled in the final pot.

The players sat for a moment or two, while the stunned group of watchers remained rooted to the spot.

Then the man with the bald head said, "Reverend, it is a pleasure to play cards with you, but . . ."

He stopped cold, obviously catching the different expression in Stillox's formerly innocent face, not to mention the appearance of two large men who looked exactly alike—down to height, width, muscle, and certainly the tight lips and cold eyes that covered the players at the table.

"Thank you, gentlemen," the Reverend Stillox said. "I am new in town. Just came in with the wagon train and with my two friends here. I'm sure glad to meet you." And with a smile that would have melted a glacier, he rose to his feet, put on his big Stetson, nodded in the direction of Clint Adams, and walked to the bar. "My offer of drinks is still open, gents. I'd like to get to know you."

SIX

It wasn't difficult finding the camp. When he rode around the high cutbank at Crazy Man Creek, there it was on a high rise of ground protected by cottonwood and box elder and willow. Approaching across the plain, Clint immediately caught the dancing sunlight on the thick goldenrod.

Presently, he saw the smoke rising from the lodge smoke holes, heard the tinkle of grazing bells in the pony herd, and it all brought a familiar tug inside him. It had been a while since he'd visited an Indian camp, and he realized now how much he had missed the experience.

The lodges were set in the accepted horseshoe shape, open eastward to face the rising sun. And the bluebirds were darting in and out of the yellow flowers. There was no game to be seen, nor any buffalo chips, which had once been so necessary for the fires. Indeed, the Gunsmith noted once again that the bark of the cottonwood trees had not been rubbed off by the buffalo scratching themselves. Another sorry sign of the rapid disappearance of the great herds.

The Sioux camp was surprisingly still. Usually there would be a great deal of activity, lots of movement and laughter, with the children running about, playing and fighting with mud balls. The bigger boys often wrestled at war games, while the women washed clothes or were engaged in sewing. This day, Clint saw hardly any of the dogs that were always present at an Indian camp. The lone barking of a single dog made the absence of others even more noticeable and at the same time filled him with something he didn't like.

As he rode in now on the big black gelding, a few of the Sioux who happened to be within sight stood still, staring at him boldly; others simply didn't look at him at all, while the women appeared to be carved like statues; and the children hid their faces.

Suddenly three warriors on horseback were in front of him and he drew rein, holding up his right hand with the palm out, the sign of peace.

"I am Adams," he said. "I come to see Chief Running Arrow."

"We see you come, long way." It was the Sioux in the middle who spoke, signing at the same time.

"I know," Clint said. "I come in peace. To talk with Running Arrow."

The man who had spoken was looking at him quietly, obviously sizing him up. His companions were as still as he was. None of them moved except when their horse moved, and then it was as though each were a part of the animal.

At last the Indian who had spoken signed for Clint to follow, and he turned his horse and started into the trees from which they had emerged. His companions flanked Clint as they rode into the camp.

Riot McTeague was a man who did not appreciate being disturbed when he was busy with something he particularly wanted to be busy with. At the present instance he'd been busy with Angie when the knock came on the door.

"Who and what?" he called out in a surly tone.

"It's Bill Gander, Mr. McTeague. L. T. told me to let you know the Englishman's been seen down by the bridge, crossing the river at Dunstan's."

"Keep an eye on him," McTeague said. Tell Moses I'll be with him shortly."

"Yes, I will."

He listened to the steps moving quickly down the corridor outside his room.

"Good thing we'd just finished," the girl said, her eyes moving slowly over his strong naked body.

"Man doesn't even get time for some ass these days, for Christ sake. What the hell's the world coming to!"

She giggled. Lifting herself up from the couch on which they'd just finished lovemaking, she rolled over and grinned at him.

They were in his office at the Double Bar Cross and had spent a happy afternoon in the pursuit and accomplishment of their mutual pleasure.

"We'll have to get going," he said. "They'll be here in a while."

"Very well." And she rose, turned her back to him, and began to pull on her clothes.

She had her underclothes on and was bending over to pull on her stockings with her back to him when she heard his step behind her, and suddenly his erection was stabbing her in the rear. In the next moment he had her on the floor, while both began pulling off her clothes.

He was a stocky gentleman in his forties, and he wore a set of bronze whiskers and mustache, a style brought into fashion by General Ambrose Burnside of the Union Army. True to the fashion of the burnside coiffure, the gentleman's chin was cleanshaven. The whiskers were precisely barbered and in fact set off his green eyes, which had a lynxlike cast to them. As a boy at school in the Old Country, he had often been cast in the role of villain in the inevitable theatrical productions that were supposed to be a part of the social upbringing and education of the proper English gentleman. His name was Cecil Cuttlebone. Indeed, *Sir* Cecil.

At the moment he was wearing a deerstalker cap, the kind of tweed cap with a bill or visor in the front and also in back and with the ear flaps tied together at the crown. Around his lumpy shoulders he wore a tweed mantle. He carried leather gloves, and his feet were encased in black, beautifully polished Wellington boots.

He was accompanied by a small party of about a dozen retainers, mostly trappers and long hunters, and there were porters for handling his numerous rifles, his special tent, his cases of liquid refreshment and numerous special foods.

One of the men was a French chef, another a trusted family retainer filling the twin offices of butler and valet. After all, Sir Cecil was roughing it.

It took Riot McTeague only a brief moment to take in the scene that greeted him as he stepped out of his front door.

The gentleman was well equipped, no doubt about it: horses, dogs, wagons, and numerous rifles—muzzleloaders, shotguns, innumerable pistols, and a couple of Sharps breechloaders. McTeague swiftly saw what care had been taken in satisfying the Englishman's hunger for sport and his reliance on the luxuries of life. There was more to the entourage, but he had seen enough to feel the tenor of the situation. Riot McTeague fooled a lot of people who thought he was an insensitive bully, overlooking his unique subtlety. It was this combination of brute force, glacial thinking, and an extremely sensient relationship with his surroundings that included not only physical appearances but people and situations that had brought him to his present status and spurred him to even further colorful adventures.

"You put me in mind of that famous Irishman Sir George Gore," he said, after greeting Sir Cecil. "Do you know about him?"

"The chap that slaughtered nearly all the buffalo singlehanded? Yes, I have heard a good bit about him. But I'm not in that game, McTeague. Just a little easy, quiet hunting is what I'm after."

"Well, come on in and we'll talk," McTeague said. "Tell your men they can get some grub at the cook shack. I've been expecting you, Cecil." McTeague slapped him cordially on the back, to the delight of his retinue, and simply made himself at home with his visitor, dropping the title or anything else that suggested obsequiousness.

Inside the living room, McTeague seated himself in an armchair and waved his guest to another.

"What'll it be? Whiskey? Got some good stuff in from Frisco. And that box there is cigars."

"Whiskey would hit the spot indeed."

For a few moments McTeague busied himself pouring the drinks, lighting his own cigar, and generally settling into his role of host, which he invariably enjoyed.

"But you know, Cecil . . . By the way, is that what they call you? Cecil? I never heard of a name like that before."

Sir Cecil gave a laugh at that. "It's common enough back home. But you can call me Seal; that's what my friends call me. And I'll call you Mac."

Looking up, McTeague saw the glint in his guest's eye and for a moment was caught in a slight surprise. But only for a moment. And he was glad for the moment, discovering that the Englishman was not as he had supposed from first glance. Of course, nobody was, but most Englishmen in the West were almost invariably classified as dudes and tenderfeet; which in fact they were. But Cecil—Seal—well, there seemed something going on there in that man. And rather than being taken aback, Riot McTeague, who had killed men with his bare hands, was intrigued.

"Have another drink, Seal," he said, as he saw how his guest polished off that well-filled glass of whiskey.

Running Arrow had been alone in his lodge when the Gunsmith was shown in. Now Clint sat opposite the chief over a low fire of buffalo chips. The chief did not speak. He had taken the traditional pipe from its resting place in front of him and was now loading it carefully with tobacco. Taking a small chip from the fire, he lighted the pipe. Then he passed it to his visitor. For some moments they smoked in absolute quiet.

Whenever Clint had smoked in the past in this way with an Indian he had never failed to feel the special weight of the moment. Without question, it was something he had never experienced anywhere else. One tribal leader had told him it was a moment of sacred time. "A time that is beyond time," was how he had put it.

This time now with Running Arrow touched the Gunsmith in the same way. It was as though time had stopped or that there was no time. He felt the whole of himself in that moment. He had wondered in the past if the tobacco had a drug in it; but he was sure not. No, there was something in the man sitting across from him, something in the very atmosphere that called something in himself. He didn't understand it, but he told himself he didn't have to. After all, he was a white, not an Indian. And he knew very well how some of the Indian chiefs were special men, men such as Crazy Horse and Sitting Bull, Cochise and Joseph, and others. He knew, too, that in the silence that was penetrating the two of them the chief was feeling him, taking him in, letting their energies mix so that there would not be simply himself and the other as two separate entities, but himself and the other as well as a third thing—their relationship. And he felt this very strongly now as he sat with Running Arrow. So that there were three forces there: himself, Running Arrow, and the combination of them both, which made them one. An old halfbreed scout and trapper had helped him understand this years before when he had visited an Atsina chief and been puzzled.

"Now we can speak with straight words," the Indian said when he had finished smoking and put down the pipe. "For we have smoked, and men cannot lie when they have smoked together." Clint was impressed by his command of English.

"I am glad of that, Running Arrow, for there is something that I wish to ask you."

The chief was looking at him but said nothing; he simply waited.

"Not yet one whole moon ago, some warriors of the Sioux were fighting with a white man's wagon train—eleven wagons not far from here at Little Wood River. I came there when they were fighting and I watched with the glasses that see far."

"You say that those warriors were from Running Arrow's people?"

"I don't know whose warriors they were. I am asking if you know of this."

"The Lakota are at peace with the white man," the chief said, using the more true name for his people. "Yet there are many bands of Lakota, those you call Sioux."

"The fighting was not far from your camp."

"There are also times when the young men cannot stand being held back, as prisoners on our own land. The young men have nothing to do. There is no longer game for hunting. And being idle brings unhappiness, which makes young men restless." He raised his head slightly, and his eyes were now looking just above his visitor. The silence was overwhelming.

"Were white people killed?" he asked; then he answered himself: "No. No one was killed or even wounded."

"That is true," Clint said.

"A horse was killed," the Indian told him, with his eyes in the same place. He lowered his head now and looked at Clint directly. "Those warriors were young men who did not wish to stay here as prisoners. They had been told many times by the elders that it was foolish to fight the white men. For there are too many of them. And that the important thing is for our people to survive, no matter how bad one feels."

"I agree with that, Running Arrow."

"There is something else you want to know," the chief said.

"I believe that there were some rifles in the whiteman wagons, rifles that were probably in a case; maybe more than one case—a big box."

The chief was silent, looking into the atmosphere. A long moment passed, and Clint was thinking of opening the conversation again, when Running Arrow spoke.

"I have something to say to you: The white men have put the poison all around us here at Crazy Man Creek."

"Poison!"

"The kind the men who follow after the buffalo leave. The pieces of poison for the wolves."

"And you say they have left some around your camp?"

"In many places, in the bodies of buffalo, sheep,

whatever one they have to kill and leave the poison in for the wolves."

"But there are hardly any wolves around," Clint said, shocked at what he was hearing from the chief, who told it dispassionately, without anger—or at least without any anger showing.

"Has any of the poison been eaten?"

"Two dogs are dead. And then who knows when some person might eat some of that meat. We do not get our food promised us by the agent man, and so the people search for food when they are hungry. A day ago Long Walking brought a piece of meat that one of his dogs had eaten. He could have brought it for himself and those in his lodge. They have been hungry, as all of us have been hungry, and they could have eaten."

"Wolf poison!"

"The gray men brought it. I am sure of that. Two of the gray men were seen, but they ran away fast on their horses."

"They were the wolfers—I'll bet on that."

"Wolfer?"

"The wolfer is a man who follows after the buffalo hunters and skinners and leaves poison for the wolves. Then he sells the wolf's pelt for a lot of money."

"I know this. But there are no wolves left here. There are no buffalo and now nearly no dogs."

There was another silence, and at last the chief said, "Small Talker and Raven want to fight the whites. And the people are listening to them. They want to rub out all the whites. I tell them no, we must live with the white man. Only my heart is not with that. My head knows we cannot beat the white man. Yet we cannot live like prisoners, like animals to be poisoned. I have long wished for peace. I have promised the white-man agent that I will keep peace, but it is hard. If my people wish to fight, then I will have to fight. I will fight with them. But our people will all be killed. And our life will be no more."

"I will find out about the poison, Running Arrow. I give my word to you."

"Can I believe the word of a white man?"

Clint Adams held the Indian chief's look. "You can believe mine, Running Arrow."

"You will stop the poison?"

"I will find out who is doing it and do all I can to stop it. That I promise."

"You will tell the army man? I have already told the agent, and he said he would tell the pony-soldier captain. But the poison is still there."

"I promise you, Running Arrow, that I will do everything I can to find out who is doing it and I will tell them it must be stopped."

The Indian was looking at him with his steady eyes. "I see that you wish to," he said. "I see that."

"And the rifles?"

"They were taken by my warriors, are you saying?"

"I do not know. I don't know if there really were rifles, but I am almost sure. I suspect it. I suspect that the fight with that small band of Sioux was staged."

"Staged?"

"Staged means it was fake. False. Not a real fight, but pretending."

"Aah!"

"Because there were no casualties."

When the chief looked puzzled, Clint said, "No one was killed or even wounded. Only that horse, which was an accident, I was told. One of the white men shot the horse by mistake. Also, none of the whites were hit."

"I find out," Running Arrow said. "You come again. We will talk about the guns and the poison. Come soon." He held up one finger and made a circle with it in front of him. Then he made a second circle and a third."

"Three days," Clint said. "I will come."

He looked again into the chief's face and saw that he had closed his eyes. Running Arrow sat as though carved into the atmosphere. He seemed to be hardly breathing as he remained, wrapped in silence.

The meeting was ended.

The Reverend Joseph Stillox had by now made it plain that the wagon train was staying in Willow Crossing. "We can settle here just as good as anywhere else," he said. "I mean, just as *well* as anywhere else," he quickly added, remembering that, as a "man of God," he was supposed to speak proper English.

Nobody appeared to object; that is, all the members began making arrangements to settle in Willow Crossing or nearby.

The Gunsmith had certainly long since figured that this had been Stillox's aim all along, and he even wondered how many of the train members were part of Stillox's plan—meaning that from the start of their journey Willow Crossing had been their real destination. And now, watching the various members of the wagon train locate themselves in town, he began to see which ones had been part of Stillox's scheme all along and which had not.

It was obvious that Molly Durham was what she said she was. He believed her story that she had joined the wagon train in order to find out who had killed her husband. He wondered whether she still felt that the man was with the group. Ever since she'd told him her story, he had been going over the travelers in his mind, weighing each one as a possibility. None seemed likely, yet that did not deter his speculation. He had known killers who on the surface appeared to be far removed from such violence. It could be anyone, he decided; and he even wondered if it had been a woman. But this really seemed too unlikely, and he dropped the notion. It had to be a man, and he finally settled on two areas of suspicion. One, the twins. The other, the mysterious scout who had disappeared, Hank Burroughs. He had questioned some of the members of the wagon train about Burroughs but come up with exactly nothing. A quiet man, kept to himself, did his job—this was the general feeling.

"He was a man who kept his nose clean," was how Oleander Hildebrand put it as they had a drink at the Inside Straight Saloon & Gaming Parlor & Dance Palace.

Clint had been nursing a beer at the bar, now and again exchanging cryptic comments with Chrome, the bartender, when he'd seen Hildebrand approaching him in the big mirror behind Chrome's chunky head and heavy shoulders. And as he saw the man coming toward him, he felt something like a surge of hope spring up that maybe, at long last, here was someone from that strange collection of travelers who might—just might—have something to offer that could help him.

"Like to buy you a drink, Adams," the man who had been a pie-eating champion said. "Got to take a leak; I'll be back. All right?"

Clint nodded. Turning around to face the big room, he leaned his elbows on the bar and let his eyes roam over the card and dice players, the faro dealer, the casual drinkers and the earnest ones; a group that was as motley as any group in any saloon in the Western country.

In a moment Oleander Hildebrand had returned, and without a word Clint led him to an empty table at one side of the room.

The Gunsmith came right to the point. "Hildebrand, I have got a strong notion that while you might well be the champion pie eater of whatever-the-hell town you mentioned back in Indiana someplace, you're also a lot of something else besides."

The knobby little man was almost grinning, looking kind of careful as he did so. His face was very wrinkled, and he had long gutters running down each side of his nose.

"Actually, I bin working for a newspaper," Hildebrand said. "The *Territorial Enterprise*, and I—"

"That is horseshit," the Gunsmith said.

"That is so. The stories are in fact mostly horseshit. A lot of it gets made up. Like the one a fellow newspaperman wrote up on the fight between Pete Gabriel and that other feller, Joe Gilligan."

"I'd say you have got the smell of the law about you," Clint said. "A whole lot stronger than printer's ink."

The grin on Hildebrand's face seemed to Clint to become even more bland.

"Do not put down such things as newspapers and pie-eating contests. They are the very backbone of this great country. The one, the great voice of the people; the other, the great coming together of the people in play, competition, and the will of all healthy countrymen to excel. I speak, of course, of that great American Pastime, the pie-eating contest, which takes place inevitably and endlessly in all of the smaller towns, villages, and hamlets of the nation. It is in such an event as a pie-eating contest that the people come together in healthy, even noble activity."

Clint decided to go along with him for a spell, for he could see that in fact Hildebrand was beginning to be open. There was no point in forcing him.

"I am interested," the Gunsmith said, "in how come you picked pies and the eating of pies as the field in which you wished to have your name go down in history."

"Could have been my mother," Oleander Hildebrand said. "Ma." He sniffed and ran his index finger along the edge of his left ear. "Ma made the best dinged apple pie ever tasted by man or boy! I mean what I am saying there!"

The Gunsmith grinned appreciatively.

His companion lifted his glass, held it in front of his eyes as though looking for something, then lowered it. "I was just remembering the time I gave up eating pies."

"You mean you quit? You stopped eating pies?"

Hildebrand nodded. "That I did. You want to know why." This last remark was not put as a question but as a statement. Clint nodded, almost unnecessarily.

"Couple of smart-alecks did me the dirty one time. Up in Bannack it was. There was a big thing going. Fourth of July. And of course they had to have all the stuff, like bobbing for apples and three-leg racing. And for sure they had to have the pie eating."

"The one who ate the most pies . . ." Clint started to say, but his companion interrupted him.

"No. Nope." He shook his head several times from side to side vigorously, as though wiping something away. "Not that kind. See, you notice I have got big jaws. The real pie contestant has to have big jaws."

"You mean, you see how many pies you can bite through at once?"

"That is so. Now see, that is how come I am the champion. Champion, I want to tell you, Adams, not only of Upper Sandusky, which happens to be the main place for the farmer's markets and Fourth of July celebrations and all like that in that part of Indiana, but a champeen elsewhere, too. Why, I won the contest out in St. Joe and up in Bannack the year before my accident. The son-of-a-bitch who done that, I'd like to have his balls!" And his face darkened.

"What did they do?" Clint asked, fully interested now.

"Well, shit, I was going along just fine. Bit through five pies, which the last feller did but had trouble. So we were tied for the champeenship. Well, this feller—his name was Mole, Polhemus Mole—he couldn't make it. He gave up."

"So you won?"

"I still had to bite through the sixth pie, on account of we had tied for five."

"Right."

"Well, I got ready, and they brought in the sixth pie and I took and bit into all six!" Suddenly Oleander Hildebrand grabbed his jaw, his face creased in severe pain.

"What happened?" Clint asked, alarmed.

"I busted damn near my whole mouthful of teeth is what happened! Some smart son-of-a-bitch had left the tin pie plate in amongst those six pies!"

"Holy Moses!" the Gunsmith muttered, overcome with awe.

"Good thing I wasn't packing any hardware!"

"You knew who did it?"

"No. But I was ready to shoot up the whole damn town, let me tell you!"

"Did you ever find out?"

"Everybody said it was a mistake."

"Well, was it?"

"I reckon it was a mistake. But shit, you know how it is: When you're that mad you just got to find somebody to blame for it! And whether or not that person did something doesn't matter."

"I do know," Clint said.

"Anyway, so that's how come I retired. Gave up my championship."

He sighed and leaned back in his chair, his eyes on Clint, who was sure he discerned a wicked twinkle.

"You're figuring on staying in Willow Crossing, I see," Hildebrand said after a moment.

"For a spell. I have to see how the gunsmithing business goes."

WAGON TRAIN TO HELL

"I have heard of you, Mr. Gunsmith," said Hildebrand, rubbing his jaw hard, as though he were massaging it. "I understand you are very fast with a gun and also that you do good gun work." He looked quickly around the room—but, Clint noted, with care. Then, leaning forward, he suddenly brought out a six-gun from inside his coat. Clint had already noticed the bulge and had added that perception to his growing store of information on Oleander Hildebrand.

"I have been looking for a man who knows his business to file this gun down so's it'll be a repeater."

Clint reached over and accepted the Colt single-action revolver that Hildebrand offered him.

"It's old reliable," Hildebrand said, "excepting it takes two men and a boy to operate. Like you likely know."

Clint nodded. "Sure do. By the time you wrestle that spring back so's the hammer can be drawn to full cock and the trigger spring is overpowered so's to release the hammer, you might as well start paying for your coffin."

"What they call an antique," Hildebrand said blandly.

Clint was inspecting the weapon, wondering why the man was carrying such an old model. It was the kind of gun you might expect to find on some old-timer, a trapper or prospector.

"I can reduce that spring tension," he said, "and file away the shoulders on the hammerlock. Might be good enough so the trigger action would be close enough to a hair's weight. Would that do you?"

Hildebrand nodded. "I reckon so."

"On the other hand, I could slip-hammer it. Tie

back the trigger or remove it, so you can draw the hammer back to full cock with your thumb. Course, that'd be at the expense of accuracy. Like you likely know."

Again the other man nodded. He picked up the gun that Clint had put down on the table and in one smooth movement holstered it beneath his wide coat.

The Gunsmith was quick to appreciate the speed and dexterity of Oleander Hildebrand's movements.

All the time they had been in conversation, Clint had noted how Hildebrand kept part of his attention on the barroom. Each time someone moved or came in or left the saloon, the man was aware of it. But his vigilance was quick and neat and would hardly have been noticed by anyone other than a man with the Gunsmith's powers of observation.

Clint had also been aware of a certain tension growing in Hildebrand, and during the silence that now enveloped them he could feel that the man was getting ready to speak further.

"About time you and me found us a place where we can talk more quiet," he said, heading Hildebrand off; and he watched the other man stifle his surprise.

"Two minds with one thought," Hildebrand said.

The Gunsmith got to his feet. "Saves time," he said. And he let Oleander Hildebrand follow him out of the saloon.

SEVEN

"I must say, Riot old boy, that your hospitality is more than even the most persnickety individual could ask for." And Sir Cecil Cuttlebone raised his glass once again in toast to his host, Riot McTeague.

"Glad you come by, Seal, glad you come by." McTeague's face was as flushed as his visitor's. They had both been addressing themselves nobly to the bottle that the rancher had brought to the table.

Each had lunched well, furthermore, and they had found a mutual interest in telling stories of their various adventures. And now, in a strange way, the rough, brawny, brawling rancher and the suave Britisher had obviously reached a common ground, the path to which had clearly been washed with generous quantities of whiskey and now brandy.

Angie had prepared the meal, with help from the cook, and she had even joined them for dessert.

Fresh game, hominy, onions, and then blueberry flapjacks, plus a bottle of a very fine red wine that Sir Cecil had sent for in his baggage. Meanwhile, his men were taken care of elsewhere, minus, of course, the alcoholic refreshment.

Interestingly, while both men had taken on quite a quantity of liquor and wine—and at moments had reached that place of the most genial conviviality, promoted as a rule through imbibing strong spirits and wines—both were now suddenly quite sober, as Riot McTeague again offered cigars, and this time Cecil accepted.

They sat in easy chairs, away from the bountiful table, and enjoyed their cigars, while Angie and a servant removed the dishes.

Sir Cecil, looking even more plump than when McTeague had first encountered him, had closed his eyes, as though he were falling asleep. McTeague was on the point of awakening him when a slight snore broke from his guest's nose and he awoke with a start.

"Ah! Sorry, old boy! Rude of me to drift off like that. It's just that your victuals were so delicious that a nap was called for. However..."

Before McTeague could say anything to that, or bring up what he had in mind, there was a knock at the door.

"Come!" he called out.

The door opened. He had expected Angie, but he was to be disappointed. An extraordinary individual stood on the threshold: short, thin, dressed in fringed buckskins that were not only too big for him but filthy; under an enormous hatbrim, out of which two large pieces had evidently been chewed; with a big six-shooter strapped to his right side, an equally impressive Bowie knife at the other; and with long, ropelike dark brown hair coming down to his narrow shoulders equaled only by the extraordinary whiskers for its chaotic effect. The man—rather, the individual—had to be a travesty of the noble mountain man, scout, and trapper of the Great West. His entry into the McTeague inner sanctum was accompanied by a very strong odor, the kind that defies both nomenclature and description.

Although in that first moment no one spoke, an uneasy silence seemed to have accompanied the astonishing figure, two of whom could have fit into those bulky clothes.

Suddenly a hole appeared in that mass of hair. McTeague thought he saw two or perhaps three brown fangs, and the person spoke.

"Lord, I got the whole shebang tied down, meanin' the hosses and men is all ready to move out. You just say the word, and I'll give the order to haul ass!"

These words were accompanied by what appeared to be a big grin, though most of the person's face was hidden. Yet the eyes lit up. They were a very pale blue, watery, with deep red gutters beneath them. Yet they were eyes that didn't miss a whisker; Riot McTeague took full note of that. But something stirred his memory.

"Why, you're . . ." he started to say.

"Paris Tbalt, himself. Why, you recollect me. Everybody does. Th'only scout-trapper-mountain man that has survived this close to the next century. Paris Tbalt he has seen it all! I mean, *all*! Same time," he continued, smacking his lips, "same time, you gents are speaking to the oldest trapper that is not yet extinct. One hunnert years and thirty-three days old, and still climbing the girls, young feller. Still mounting 'em!"

"Scout Tbalt!' Cecil Cuttlebone suddenly burst out. "You are definitely out of order! You are in Mr. McTeague's house and, moreover, in my company, so you will be good enough to comport yourself in the required manner."

Apparently the old scout's jaw fell, for his beard dropped down almost to his belly, which was round, even though he was thin, and protruded like the underside of a bowl. "Damnit to hell, Lord, you know I can't understand that fancy talk of yourn. I ast you more'n once to speak in simple words. Plus I know damn well whose house I am in. I have knowed Right Tigg from the time he was wet behind his ears and still peein' free of wearing any pants."

At which point McTeague lost control of himself and burst into a guffaw of delighted laughter, to the obvious distress of Sir Cecil, who was trying to maintain order and impose discipline. Even so, Cuttlebone was equal to the moment, refusing to give ground under the barrage of high humor.

"Tbalt! You are in my employ!"

"What the hell do that mean, Lord?"

"It means I pay you, board and found, or whatever the devil your American Western expression is for the simple act of weekly emolument! I pay the price and I call the turn. Now then, state your message and remove yourself and that unbelievable smell that you have brought with you into this good person's presence!"

The old scout looked as though he had been struck

by lightning. His beard and chin sagged, his mouth opened, his hands seemed to carve the atmosphere around him in search of firm support. Finally his eyes centered on Riot McTeague. "Mr. Right Tigg, sir, will you tell this kindly old scout just what'n hell that Lord feller is sayin'! Can't the feller speak American, or 'leastways English?"

McTeague, who had hardly recovered from his furious bout of laughter, managed to firm his voice sufficiently to say, "He is telling you to leave, Paris. And stop calling me Right Tigg. You have known me from way back and you know damn well that is not my kind of name." All laughter had left him now as he finished his sentence.

"Then what monicker are you favorin'?" Paris Tbalt asked.

"That is a real dumb question, Paris, even for you. Now, why don't you shut up and do what the gentleman here says. Otherwise he's likely to cut those fancy galluses you're wearing to hold up those lead pants."

"Won't matter a ding-dong!" the old scout crowed. Then he cackled. "On account of I got me a belt to make sure them things stays up!" He belched suddenly, lacing the surrounding atmosphere with the smell of trail whiskey, and he showed that, indeed, he was wearing a rope belt to make sure his pants stayed up.

By this point Sir Cecil Cuttlebone had completely recovered from his momentary annoyance. Indeed, as McTeague had already begun to suspect, he was fond of the old scout. This fact was now revealed in his lordship's offer of a drink from the bottle of wine he had brought.

"Don't mind if I do," Paris said, beaming and moving his jaw fast, like a prairie dog chewing on something good, and at the same time wiggling his beard, shaking his head, and digging deep into his crotch, evidently to locate an itch.

McTeague produced another glass and poured generously. He didn't mind the interruption. He wanted to take his time with Cuttlebone, for he had a question nagging at him: Why was Cuttlebone out here in this part of the country? The land was trapped out and hunted out. Everybody knew that. And still, here was the great European hunter, just like that grand duke or Lord or whatever the hell he was who'd come out to the Black Hills with Custer and a whole collection of sports. Or was it that the English were just so God-damn dumb? Coming out to the West and buying up land and running cattle companies from way back in England, treating everybody like they were nothing. He watched Paris Tbalt down his glass of powerful red wine like it was water, and he almost laughed out loud at the alarm in Cecil Cuttlebone's face.

"By the Lord Harry, Tbalt, you treat wine like it was sarsaparilla or some wretched drink like that! Don't you realize, man, that you are imbibing vintage stock!"

Paris Tbalt's prominent brown teeth sprang into view as he grinned. "By God, Lord, that red stuff there puts me in mind for a crack at some of the girls! Bin a while since I have had a chance to dip my wick, I got to tell you!"

"Well now, Paris, you may withdraw. We shall let you know our next move. Stay close. Keep alert.

And above all, stay sober! You know that I will not tolerate drunkenness on the job!"

Cackling and scratching into his behind, the old scout stepped lickety-split to the door, opened it, and, with a great sigh, departed.

Silence fell. It was clear to both men that the room without the rambunctious Paris Tbalt was less. But both would very likely have agreed that, in the present case, less had to be better than more.

"That man can wear one out," commented Sir Cecil, his eyes on the ceiling as though searching for help. "But I am told he is a good scout, and in fact I rather like him at times, despite his ridiculous behavior." He dropped his eyes now to his host.

Riot McTeague got up, walked to the door, and locked it. Then he walked back to his chair and sat down.

"We'll talk now," McTeague said. "I figure you've got news for me."

"That I have. I have indeed."

"I'm listening."

As Clint Adams shortly discovered when he visited Miller's Tunnel Saloon with Oleander Hildebrand, the new establishment was a good bit more than its name implied. It was a huge place, sporting five monte tables, each six-by-four feet, with the building itself sixty feet long and twenty wide. The location was perfect: Everyone entering town had to pass Miller's Tunnel Saloon. Equipment had been shipped from the East. The bar was among the first made of mahogany ever to appear in that part of the country. It was thirty feet long and ran along the east side of the room. The furniture was of top quality, including four huge crystal chandeliers that held coal-oil lamps.

"Don't tell me who owns this place," Clint said as they found a table at which to sit with their drinks. "Let me guess."

Hildebrand grinned at him. "The same feller owns everything just about in Willow Crossing."

"McTeague is a smart one to open up his own competition."

Hildebrand's look became dead serious. "He's a smart one at anything."

Clint studied the room while they got used to their drinks for a few moments.

"I get the feeling they're running straight games," he said, speaking to his companion, but with his eyes still covering the big room.

"Like I said, McTeague is a smart one."

"You know him? I mean, from before?" Clint asked, wondering if the other man's give-away had been intentional.

"Let's say that I have heard of him."

Clint said nothing but kept his attention on the room and its clientele. He had heard that Miller's had set limits to be bet on monte, faro, the wheels of fortune, and blackjack. There was no chance for any player to double up on his bets. Clever. The average player, a cowboy or miner, never had enough cash to buck the almost unlimited resources of such an establishment. At McTeague's Inside Straight it was different. There you could bet your britches.

As Clint well knew, monte and faro were the two most popular gambling games in the West. For a while now he watched the nearest monte game, with its two dealers: one to pass out the cards and the other to pull in the money. The simplicity of the game, and the fact that it appeared to give the player an even break, was what made it popular. Of course, it was a variation of the bunco artist's shell game.

He turned his attention to the faro game now, since Hildebrand seemed also to be interested in his surroundings. Clint had definitely decided not to push things.

Each of the two men had come close to the bottom of his glass when Hildebrand finally spoke.

"Interesting place," he said. "And, like I say, it shows Mr. McTeague to be a cut ahead of his customers."

"I have heard McTeague's changed the whole town," Clint said. "Build it up from a bunch of soddies."

"Likewise," Hildebrand said solemnly. "I have heard the very same."

"Willow Crossing 'pears to be the kind of town where a man could throw his bedroll and settle in.'" Clint's tone was casual, leaving the other man plenty of room not to answer.

"Maybe," Hildebrand said. "If a man's got a family. For myself, I dunno. Had a wife . . ." He dropped his voice slightly as he pulled his chair a little closer to the table. "But she got the croup and up and died. How come I joined Stillox—sort of like to get away. Had a spread—small, five hundred head—down by Lander. Sold up when Nellie went West. Then I heard tell of Stillox's train coming through, so I joined it. Had to do all my own driving. But I didn't mind, though I never got much sleep."

"He went by Lander?"

"I picked him up at Laramie."

"Yeah." Clint nodded, remembering that that was where Molly Durham had joined Stillox. "I heard some others took on at Laramie," he said easily.

"That feller Hank."

"The scout?"

Hildebrand nodded. They had brought the bottle to the table, and he reached out now and poured into both glasses. He appeared to be giving this simple job his full attention, but Clint knew he had to be thinking of how the conversation was going; as, indeed, he was doing himself.

"Hank Burroughs," Hildebrand said thoughtfully. "Now, how do you figure a man like that got tied into an outfit like Stillox and those twins were running? The twins, let me add, which I haven't seen much of since we got to town."

"I haven't either," Clint said. "But, getting back to your first question about Hank Burroughs throwing in with Stillox and those two, well, I dunno. I never met Burroughs. All I know is what people, two or three in the wagons, said about him—that he was a good man. Everybody thought it funny how come he just up and pulled out."

"That they did," Hildebrand said. "And real sudden, it was."

"Did you get to know the man?" Clint asked. "Did you talk to him?"

Hildebrand had been looking down at his glass of whiskey. It was on the table, but he had his fingers loosely around it. He seemed to be deep in thought, and a moment went by without him saying anything in response to Clint's question.

"You said I had the look of the law about me, Adams."

Clint nodded, remembering the time and place in which he'd taken the chance and slipped in the challenging statement. He remembered too, that Hildebrand hadn't answered him.

He waited a beat and then said, "You have still got that look about you; though I am not necessarily saying you're a lawman. I'd say more a private type, like a stock detective, or maybe even a Wells, Fargo man." He spoke quietly, with a smile at the corners of his mouth.

"By God, I hope I don't give off those signs to the general population," Hildebrand said drily.

"I don't believe you do. I've had a lot of training in sizing up the law, and also the not-law," Clint said. "I used to wear one of those things on my shirt. Long time back."

"I know," Hildebrand said.

"You know?" And the rush of surprise almost took the Gunsmith off guard. But he recovered ably.

"I knew you were on your way to Willow Crossing."

"How come you knew that? The only person I told was Bill Jarnegan back in Gender Butte."

"Bill Jarnegan is an old friend of mine," Hildebrand said.

Clint Adams leaned back now, and reaching up, he pushed the brim of his Stetson so that it sat further back on his head.

"It was a surprise to me when you showed up after the Indian trouble," Hildebrand said.

"Then you must have known that Stillox was intending all along to go to Willow Crossing."

"Mitch Durham knew it," Hildebrand said, after

taking a quick glance around the room. "Molly Durham's husband."

"And got killed for his pains, did he?"

"That's what it looks like. Mitch and myself are—were—stock detectives. But I don't know what happened. Mitchell got shot up, murdered in cold blood."

"Was it Burroughs?" Clint asked.

Hildebrand was already shaking his head, having anticipated the question.

"Burroughs was with you and Durham?" said Clint, taking a wild guess.

Oleander Hildebrand nodded.

The Gunsmith allowed a few moments to fall between them as he studied the new situation. Well, it added up. But what were they really looking for? The three of them—Hildebrand, Durham, and Burroughs.

"Does Molly Durham know who you are?" he asked.

"I don't believe she does. But you never know. The only way she could suspect anything would be if Mitch had told her. And, knowing Durham, I doubt that very much."

"Then," said Clint, "I have just one more question—at least for the moment."

"You want to know what I want from you."

"I know what you want from me," Clint said, with an easy smile. "I spotted that way back."

"Then what?" Hildebrand asked, shocked into a pretty big surprise.

"I want to know if you really ever were a pie-eating champion, especially in Upper Sandusky, Indiana."

In the evening the long light of the westering sun slipped across the great plain, without any sound at all and with no disturbance to the world it was feeding; its brilliance was like a remembering touch on the land, on the ranch that seemed to be growing in the valley, with its horses, its cattle, its men.

For Riot McTeague it was the time of day he especially liked. He did not know why. Only now, as he sat facing his guest who had fallen asleep, he let his eyes wander to the window that showed the butte, the table land, the tops of the Bear Tooth mountain range against the sapphire sky, and the high, imperious eagle sweeping through the great sky that seemed to be holding the land forever.

A snore interrupted his reverie. It was not that Riot McTeague was thinking such poetic thoughts, but he was not and never had been a totally insensitive man, and he was well aware of the feeling that the lone eagle must be experiencing as he disappeared into the embrace of the great sun as it touched the tips of the Bear Tooth Mountains.

He was moved, and this made him feel uncomfortable, and so his thoughts turned to Angie. He began to feel his passion for her and wished that his company were not there. And then this association led him to thoughts of his recent conversation with Cecil Cuttlebone, as a louder, almost blistering snore rode down Sir Cecil's prominent nose and vibrated into the room.

"Actually, I am here on a mission," Cuttlebone

had said. He had sneezed then, an enormous sneeze, and hadn't been able to cover it with the silk handkerchief he had pulled magnificently from the pocket of his plaid hunting jacket.

"I figgered that," Riot had countered. "I can see from all those guns, hunters, trappers, and all the rest of it that you haven't come out here to study the wildflowers or the habits of the rattlesnake. Case you didn't know it, I am close to Thorpe McCool. I know your plan. I was expecting you."

"Oh, jolly good! Then you know good old Thorpe! Wizard!" And he had beamed all over the room, and as he reached for his glass his chubby face broke into a chuckle of pleasure.

"You're going to be hunting buffalo, McCool said."

"And elk and pronghorn antelope, and a number of other species of game," Sir Cecil said enthusiastically.

He drank, hiccuped gently, and resumed his expression of pleasure. "I am so very glad to meet a real Westerner at long last. May I ask, Riot, are you a cowboy?"

"I have been, but right now I own this spread." And he waved his hand at the window.

"But of course!" Sir Cecil rubbed his round tummy with both palms as he surveyed his host. "Good thing I realized that—I mean, in time. You see, it's damned difficult for a visitor such as myself to understand the different social strata out here in the West. I mean, how to tell the working men from their masters."

McTeague was staring at him open-mouthed. "Listen, Seal, if I were in your boots I would make damn sure I never asked any buckaroo hereabouts such a question."

"You don't say! But Riot, tell me, my good man, what would you, for instance, say if someone came up to you and asked just that question. Where is your master?"

"A feller did that once," McTeague said. "A good while back. I do believe he never did get over it."

"Why? What happened? What did he say? What did you answer him?"

"I told him the son-of-a-bitch hadn't been born yet."

It took a moment for Sir Cecil Cuttlebone to let it sink in. And then he released a great shout of laughter that all but rattled the big window and brought a great smile of relief to Riot McTeague.

"Cuttlebone, I am glad to see that you're human, after all."

"Thank you, Riot, old boy. Please don't feel it necessary to flatter me, however. I have, after all's said and done, deliberately and with a great deal of forethought come to the American West in order to rough it, and to learn the ways of the inhabitants—at any rate the white, if not the red. And in view of this, uh, position that I have taken with myself, I shall appreciate any and all help that you can offer me. In a word, Riot, have no mercy on me. Incidentally, I've heard rumors that the game, especially the buffalo, are not numerous. Is this true?" He pursed his lips and raised his thick eyebrows into an arch of concern.

Riot McTeague had grinned amiably and offered his lordship another drink. He was happy to see that the plan was going well; the plan that he and Thorpe

McCool of the Liverpool Land Management Company had worked out.

The hitching racks were crowded, so Clint decided on the livery stable, but then he spotted a place just outside the Inside Straight. He kicked Duke over to the bay and sorrel horse, and wrapped his reins loosely over the hitching pole. Then he stepped up onto the boardwalk and started toward Butterworth's General Store. He had just ridden in from scouting some of the country up around the Double Bar Cross range, and what he had seen had only emphasized to him that he was very likely going to need plenty of ammo. He always made it a point to keep his supply well filled.

A heavyset man with a lot of loose skin on his long face and wearing dark yellow galluses over a black and white striped shirt greeted him.

"I am needing some ammo," Clint said, approaching the worn wooden counter.

The storekeeper's sharp eyes flicked to the holstered .45. "For the Colt?" His damp black hair was combed close to his head; his hands were puffy, and the gunsmith noted as he leaned onto the counter, spreading his pudgy fingers, that there was no indentation between the knuckles.

"Two boxes will do me now," Clint said, "and two for the Winchester," he added, ".44-.40."

"See you about town, Mr. Adams. Glad to have a man like yerself in this part of the country here. I'm Charlie Butterworth." He didn't offer his hand, but he was deferential. He was an expansive man; his body was large, but his skin hung on his large frame like a loose sack, much bigger than his body.

Clint nodded to his salutation and said nothing. The storekeeper flushed a little.

"Quiet in town," Butterworth resumed, trying to pick things up. "Which is good enough for sure, considering there ain't been a marshal here at Willow Crossing since Torbit Anders got cut down."

"How long ago was that?" Clint asked.

Butterworth relaxed a bit then, glad the conversation was going two ways. His lips pursed; he looked like he was about to blow a bugle, Clint thought. "Since last Fourth of July."

"That's a long time for some towns to be without the law," Clint said.

"But I hear tell we're getting a new man. Mr. McTeague and the council have got somebody from that wagon train you come in with."

"Know the name, do you?"

"Didn't hear any name. But they say he's a good one."

"Good enough," the Gunsmith said, and with a nod he turned and walked out of the store.

And almost smack into Molly Durham, who was coming along the boardwalk with some packages in her arms. Only by swift action on the part of Clint Adams was disaster avoided. In the process, though, he missed his attempt to grab one sliding bundle and instead felt his hand on a very soft but at the same time firm bosom. To his great delight and to his companion's embarrassment.

"Mr. Adams!" She hissed the words as the crowd of people, heavy as it always was at that time of day, swirled past them.

"I beg your pardon," the Gunsmith said. "But I must also tell you it was my great pleasure."

"Villain!" she hissed. And they both had to stifle their laughter in order to avoid a scene right there in the center of town.

But the idea that had been ignited at that moment bore instant fruit, and fifteen minutes later they were in Molly's room at the Widow Carrington's guest house.

"Mr. Adams, will you please undress me before I tear my clothes off, and yours as well."

He slipped his arms around her then and said, "That is exactly what I was intending to do, young lady."

His fingers were already unbuttoning the long line of white buttons that rode up from her waist to her neck. But she was impatient and couldn't wait, so she began helping him.

At the same time they took some moments to kiss and embrace, rubbing their bodies against each other, so that the unbuttoning seemed endless. And by the time she was out of her dress and standing in her petticoat, his erection was almost ripping his pants open.

"I like you," she whispered as, standing by the bed, he pushed his erection between her legs. Reaching down, she pulled down her skirts and helped him out of his pants. His hands were busy with her breasts; one of them had sprung into his fingers, and he began playing with its nipple, which was erect with desire.

In the next moment they were on the bed and naked. He was running his fingers through her bush, which was a riot of brown hair and wet to his exploring touch. She had his stiff organ in her fist and was stroking it, her hand sliding wetly along him. Then she was rubbing the head of his tool right up into her slit, which was also soaking wet now from both of them.

She had spread her legs wide, with her knees up, and he mounted her, sliding easily inside, riding up high and all the way to the point where the head of his member touched her wall and she squealed with delight.

"It's so wonderful!" The words breathed against his ear and then she was kissing him, running her tongue deep into his mouth, while he returned the movement, letting his tongue play with hers as their mouths filled with saliva.

He rode her gently, firmly, but as though exploring, which he was. He was in no hurry, yet he felt her nervousness and her need to come quickly. He stroked her with long, slow motions of his organ, coming down to a slower pace, which was almost more than she could bear.

In another moment or so he began to move faster, and she kept pace with his acceleration. She was accepting him the whole way, her legs spread even wider than before, it seemed to Clint, and now he put his hands under her buttocks as she pumped and rotated herself on his rigid organ.

They stroked faster now, each drawing the full beauty out of the moment, hardly able to bear the exquisite delight that they knew was coming. She was panting, and so was he, with the delicious exertion of their tempo together. Faster now, and faster, they closed in on the astonishing apex of their great joy, and he suddenly began to pump out his come, and she met it with hers, and they moved faster, beautifully entwined, and faster and easier and smoother, until the explosion took complete possession of them and they were oblivious to all else.

Gradually they subsided and lay still, he still on top of her, with his member softer now, no longer erect and hard, but relaxed.

Together they lay in their delicious embrace. They slept. And later, when they awoke, they made love again.

EIGHT

McTeague kept two offices in town: one at the Inside Straight and the other at Miller's Tunnel Saloon. At the moment he was receiving Joe Stillox at Miller's. The office was upstairs and overlooked Main Street, with a view of the livery, the Barber and Bath Emporium, Clyde O'Fiske's Undertaking and Gravedigging Establishment, plus a few stores.

"Do you think they're gonna handle it all right then?" Stillox was saying, a gold tooth gleaming in the early morning sunlight.

"I do. Especially when they realize who the new marshal is."

"They don't suspect anything?"

Stillox was seated in the battered easy chair next to McTeague's big rolltop desk, which was a riot of papers, parts of a six-gun, an old cigar butt, and some nails and screws, plus an old rag that smelled of linseed oil.

"What is there to suspect?" demanded McTeague. "For God sake, they haven't had the law in this town since the last marshal bit the dust, so they should be looking forward to"—and he paused a second while now his voice took on a sonorous note—"the building and growth of a respectable town! A credit to the land, the country, to God!"

"You took the words right out of my mouth," said Joseph Stillox in admiration. "Riot, I think you ought to run for territorial governor."

"Do you mean that?" McTeague was suddenly serious, and Stillox congratulated himself on having hit the right note. God, it was about time. McTeague was a tough nut to crack.

"I mean that, Riot. You could go far. And there ain't—I mean, there *is*—no question of your helping the country. You've already built something here, and I see how it's growing every day. One day there'll be a city right here where we are sitting."

"I think you believe that."

"I do." His voice was solemn, as though he were taking an oath.

Riot McTeague felt a little ball of pleasure bounce through him at those two words. Well, by God, he had earned it. He had no doubt on that. He had earned every bit of it. At the same time, though, Riot McTeague had not reached his present position by being the total slave to flattery. He was basically a practical man, and so he asked a pertinent question at this point.

"What about Adams?"

"We have our eye on him."

"You and the twins?"

Stillox nodded.

"And what about that man you were telling me about—Hildebrand? What's he up to?"

"Hildebrand and Adams have had drinks together a couple of times, but no action that I can tell. Adams has his eye on the Durham woman. Don't know if he's got any further than shaking hands, but I don't believe it'll be for lack of trying if he doesn't."

"I want you to start raising money for a church. That old meetinghouse you've been using isn't good enough. We want a real church, so start hitting the tub for it."

Stillox smiled at that. "I am right with it," he said. "Raising money in the name of the Lord is right up my alley."

"Just remember that the money's for the Lord," McTeague said.

"I know you won't let me forget, Riot, old friend."

They both had a chuckle over that.

"How is Cuttlebone doing?" Stillox asked, reaching forward to take the cigar McTeague was passing him.

"Cecil is doing fine."

"He don't suspect anything? I mean to say, he *doesn't*?"

"He doesn't. But he will if he runs into you and you don't do better with your language. You're supposed to be talking like a preacher."

"Me a preacher! I've done it before. A few times, Riot. Don't worry, I'll be careful," he said quickly, as he saw McTeague's face darken. "After all," he went on. "You can't expect me to be as polished as yourself; a man who can be and has been just about anything you can name in the American West—rancher, cowboy, trapper, builder of towns, gambler, and the Lord knows what else." He spoke with admiration, and it was a true admiration that he felt.

"Just so's Adams doesn't catch on to anything," McTeague cautioned. "I have heard of that gentleman, and he is no one to rub on the wrong side. Also, I don't want Cuttlebone to get wise to why he's really out here."

"You mean what he's really hunting for," put in Stillox, brisk with eagerness as the plan that Riot had proposed long before was finally unfolding. By God, that man was a man of complex parts, a man of accomplishments. He wondered whether Riot had ever been a man of God. He thought of asking but then decided on the safer path. You couldn't always tell how McTeague was going to take things, especially questions.

But then he did blurt out something: "You know, I wonder about it with Cuttlebone."

"What do you wonder?"

"Well, just from what I pick up around town. What I hear. Everybody is saying this rich old bugger from England is out here to shoot up the wildlife and take a mess of trophies back to the Old Country." Stillox paused, looking into space as though searching something further.

"So that's what he's doing, isn't he?"

"Sure. That's what he's supposed to be doing—bagging a big kill."

"So?"

"So I have heard one or two people asking how come he figures he can do that when the country is hunted out. There are no buffalo and damn little game. What the hell is he going to shoot?" He paused and then said, "I'm just saying that that is what people are saying."

"One or two like."

"Yeah. But there could be more."

"There will be more," McTeague said, with a smile forming at the corners of his mouth. "I expect there to be a lot more with that same question." He looked squarely at Stillox. "Fancy Joe. You didn't earn that name by being dumb, Joseph. And I hope that I haven't up and hired the wrong man."

And suddenly a grin broke out all over Stillox's face. "Course, Riot. Of course. I can see it. I am following it right along. I'm just telling you—well, like I said, people are beginning to fall for it."

For a long moment Riot McTeague kept his eyes on the other man, not letting him go, wanting Stillox to know that he saw through that bull, wanting him to know he could handle him and those dumb twins any time he felt like it, wanting him to by damnit know who was boss and way ahead of him.

Satisfied at last that his point had been made, he said, "And now about the rifles."

"Raven and Small Talker have got the Spencers and are only waiting for the ammo when you give the word."

"Good. I'll be sending the wolfers out in a day or two for their second spreading. They'll butcher something or other up by Solly Creek, which isn't too far from the Sioux camp. And we should get some results. If all goes well, and I figure it will, those two Injuns will be running to us for the ammo for the Spencers."

"But they'll not be coming to town," said Stillox, keeping his voice steady. "Even though they were pretending out there with the wagons, it didn't make me feel like dancing a jig."

"They have got their orders. And Running Arrow knows nothing about any of it."

A silence fell upon the room then, and both men drank the last of the whiskey.

"That'll do 'er then, Joseph."

Stillox stood up.

"I am counting on you, Joseph, to watch Adams and to keep an eye on Hildebrand, too. I don't know who the hell he is, but if you say he's seen Adams a couple of times, then he needs to be watched. But mostly I want you to keep those two heavies in line."

"I raised Clancy and Nole from the time they were boys. They'll do just what I say, Riot." He suddenly let loose a little bark of laughter. "I'd reckon this was about the first and maybe only time there's been twin marshals running a town."

"Just see that they do a good job," McTeague said. "I don't want them doing something dumb."

"I'll handle them."

"I mean that, Joseph. I don't want them shooting up the town or trying to outdraw Adams or beating anybody up; unless, of course, they deserve it. Now, by the end of the week, I'll have the rest of the town offices filled. I'm keeping two or three old hands on the council for appearances, but I'll be heading it up. Main thing is the law, and I am counting on you and those two ironheads."

As Stillox walked to the door of the office, McTeague stood up and came around the desk.

"Come by again tomorrow, maybe the next day,"

he said to Stillox. "Unless something comes up. No later, though."

When he shut the door, he stood there listening to Stillox descending the stairs. Then he walked back to his desk and sat down.

He remained there, going over the conversation that he'd just had with Joe Stillox and feeling out his plan. Everything seemed to be going well. The only thing was that he wasn't at all sure about Adams. Well, there was nothing he could do about that now. Unless... The thought swept suddenly into his brain: insurance. Yes, it was the time for it. He had already considered it and put it aside. It wasn't good to have too many things in the fire. And what's more, that Gunsmith fellow was a dangerous number. But it would be a good idea to be sure.

He took another drag on his cigar and then dropped it into the cuspidor at the foot of his desk. Then he stood up and walked to the door of the office.

He locked the door behind him and walked down the hallway to the bedroom at the far end. She must have heard him coming, for the door was ajar.

"All done?" Angie asked as he entered the room, turned, and locked the door behind him.

"Only just beginning," McTeague said, and he turned to face her.

She was sitting on the edge of the bed, wearing a dressing gown that he had given her.

"I brought up a bottle so we could have a drink," she said. "Though maybe you don't need one." Her smile was wide open, and it brought the excitement right into the center of his belly.

"Let's just have it on hand," he said as he walked

slowly toward her. "And see what happens."

As he walked she began undressing, and by the time he'd reached her she was naked.

"I beat you to it," she said.

"Then you better give me a hand."

"I'll give you more than that," Angie said, as she leaned over and began unbuckling his belt.

In the Sioux camp there was no happiness; no young boys were throwing mud balls with the yellow sticks, nor were the older boys playing the war game of Throwing Them off Their Horses.

In Running Arrow's lodge, the chief sat with the two young warriors, Raven and Small Talker. He had filled the traditional pipe and they had smoked in silence and they had looked at each other through eyes that were like windows. At the same time, the chief, who was an old man now, knew very well that the two warriors were not wholly at ease.

He had called them to the meeting. First there had been the meeting with the elders, when the two had been spoken to about their behavior in dealing with the whites, their now-and-again raids on some of the surrounding white settlers and especially this latest thing, the dealing with the whites over the guns and the false attack on the wagon train.

The elders had been severe and had recommended turning the pair over to the dog soldiers, who would discipline them, along with those others who had been in the raiding band. There were some present who had mentioned banishment, at least for a time. There were others who'd prescribed pony whipping. But all were equal in their realization of the shame that had been brought on to Running Arrow's band.

Now the chief sat alone with the two instigators and leaders of the renegade band. All would be punished, put to shame, and pony whipped, the two leaders receiving the most; but there would be no banishment. Running Arrow had argued against it. For, he pointed out, there was enough sorrow in the tribe without casting off those who had made a mistake, even a mistake as serious as the receiving of rifles.

"The white men gave you those rifles so that then they could claim you were going to fight them," Running Arrow now told them. "Surely, you could see this."

"But they gave us no bullets," Small Talker said. "The guns would have been useless for us."

"Then you were even more foolish to accept them," Running Arrow pointed out.

"But we would have gotten the bullets from the white men," Raven said. "And then we could have used the guns."

"Against all those pony soldiers?" The chief's words were scored with scorn.

"It is so, Running Arrow." Raven spoke with his head bowed.

"You have heard the words of the elders, of Runs Quickly and Eagle Bone and the others. It is not necessary to talk more of this. You will do as the council has said. Bring the guns here and then you will receive your punishment."

A silence fell upon the lodge then. Even though the talk was obviously ended, no one immediately got up to leave, for it was also clear that Running Arrow had not yet finished.

After another long moment, the chief spoke again.

"There are the gray men with the poison. I want you to watch them. Do not let them see you. Watch where they put the poison. Follow them closely, but they must never know that you are there. And report everything you see. At the same time, no harm must come to the gray men. For they are whites, and the other whites, the pony soldiers, will say that even though they put poison for the Indian to eat, they are still to be believed and thus honored before the red man."

He became silent, but the two warriors still waited. Presently, they rose and left the lodge, while Chief Running Arrow continued to sit in exactly the same position.

After a while he rose and went outside. He walked slowly through the camp. As he passed silently, heads turned to see him. And he could feel the sadness everywhere.

Entering his lodge again, he saw that the fire had been lighted—he supposed by Little Feather, one of his young wives. He seated himself and began preparing his pipe. When the pipe was ready, he offered it to the Four Directions of the wind, and then, taking a small buffalo chip from the fire, he lighted it.

Tomorrow, he told himself, before the dawn came to light the rimrocks of the surrounding mountains, he would go to the high place that he had known for a very long time, and he would cry for help. It was a good time for that. He had not been to the high place where he had last dreamed for a long time. It seemed now a very long time.

He had closed his eyes—not to sleep, but to see better into the place where real things happened—when he felt the approach of a horse and its soft nicker. He opened his eyes as one of his warriors came to tell of the arrival of the white man Adams.

Mick Folio and his companions, Perry Ollinger and Nile Hastie, were standing at the edge of the clearing, looking at the tiny buffalo herd.

"Sure as hell you won't find no silks in that bunch," Mick said. Turning his head slightly, he placed his calloused thumb against the side of his nose and blew.

"A ratty bunch of hides, for sure," said Nile Hastie. He was a man with a long face, a derby hat, and very hairy hands. The left hand was minus its thumb.

The third man, who was taller than his companions, said nothing. Perry Ollinger was scratching himself vigorously, trying vaguely and with not too much interest to remember when he'd last had a bath; he was thinking it might be time for another, since the itching was beginning to bother him.

Mick was the chunkiest of the trio—almost as wide, it seemed to some people, as he was high. "There'll always be wolves," he said philosophically in reply to the earlier observation by one of his companions that they had about poisoned themselves out of work, having all but wiped out the wolves; and that the lack of buffalo had more than just helped the terrible state of affairs.

"Yup, I reckon so," observed Perry, still scratching.

"Well," said Nile, working his little finger up his nose to extract a clinker, "I'm for heading for Montana. It's better pickin's there, I bin told."

"Later," Mick said. "We have got business here. Remember?"

"Thing is," Nile said, "thing is, we got to be careful we don't get them fuckin' Injuns excited."

"That is for sure," Mick said. "Who's got some liquid left?"

Perry produced a squat bottle of brown fluid. "This'll put lead in your ding-dong," he said. And he winked at Mick who grinned wickedly. "I sure could use some. Sure could."

"Thing is, we got to tend to business here. That McTeague, is no man to fuck around with." Mick spat at a clump of sage as they stood at the edge of the clearing and surveyed the small herd of buffalo.

"We kin handle him," Perry said.

"He has got a big mouth," Nile added. "But he has got a cute little ding-dong woman. I seen her down to the Tunnel one time. Got a ass that's just built for play." And he cackled and rubbed his crotch affectionately.

"Listen! We have got this here to handle," said Mick. "You can handle your whanger later, but right now we got to drop one of them buffs an' gut him."

"And who's got the strychnine?" Perry asked. "I didn't bring it."

"Not me," Hastie said, and both of them looked toward Mick Folio who was checking the load in his Spencer rifle. He raised his head. "Good thing somebody here's got some brain to him," he said.

As he spoke, he kept his eyes on the buffalo he'd selected. "One shot ought to do her," he said then. "You dumb shits get your skinners ready."

He kneeled now and sighted. The buffalo, being nearsighted and also being upwind of the men, had no awareness of their presence.

"You reckon any Injuns about?" Perry asked.

"You boys keep a look-see," said Mick, and he pulled the trigger.

The men watched the bull take the bullet, sway a little, then drop to its knees. The rest of the buffalo began to mill around it.

"They'll move off when they get a whiff of us," Mick said. "When we get upwind. Then we gut him and move him up closer to the Injun camp."

"You don't figger any one of them savage bastards heard that shot?" asked Nile.

"Fuck 'em if they did," Mick snapped. "We got Spencers and what do they got?"

"They got shit," said Perry. "That's what they got."

They moved swiftly now. With their skinning knives, they gutted the carcass, then cut out the tongue to keep it. Nile Hastie brought the packhorses, and they loaded the parts they needed. Then they spread strychnine into the remaining guts of the buffalo.

"We'll leave it right here," Mick said. "And we'll take this up closer to their camp and put the poison there too.

"That it, then?" Perry asked.

Nile said, "He wanted more. I do believe our leader here told us," and he turned a sneering face toward Mick.

Mick, who had been tightening the cinch on his saddle horse, dropped his hands and turned toward Nile Hastie.

"You want your guts gutted too, do you?" And in a flash, the glittering blade of his skinning knife appeared in his hand.

"Just funnin' a little, Mick," Nile said quickly. "No need to get a hard-on about it."

"Keep yer fuckin' mouth shut then."

Nile said nothing, and Perry began studying the terrain ahead of them.

"We will head up toward the camp."

"Crazy Man Creek?"

"That is what I just said." And Mick kicked his roan into an easy walk. "C'mon, you crowbait. You got a lot more miles to go 'fore you lie down for good."

The sky had clouded over suddenly while they were putting out the poison and securing the rest of the buffalo carcass to the bay packhorse. Now, as they rode out of the clearing, a thin drizzle began to fall.

"Fuckin' rain!" Mick Folio muttered with venom. He spat furiously at a small rock. "I also got me a creepy feeling that maybe we ain't all that much alone."

Dawn had come gently to the tawny plain. It didn't make a sound, and nothing was disturbed but only touched in that secret way that is understood by those who realize that all life is one. In silence the night had again retreated. And all at once it was day; the bronze morning light began stroking the lodges at Crazy Man Creek, the camp of Running Arrow's band. A dog barked, while the pungent smell of burning buffalo chips, lifting off the cookfires, reached into the fresh, wet air that had not yet departed with the night. It had rained during the night, but now it was a new day, fresh with a new visibility.

The new sun was above the horizon now, its light

touching the drops of water that remained on the grass and branches of the trees. A flock of chickadees flew suddenly over the pony herd, and a blue jay called. Running Arrow, returning to his lodge, caught the tinkle of a grazing bell.

More than thirty winters, he was thinking, since the first wagon train of emigrants was seen on what became spoken of by the Wasichus as the Oregon Trail. And Thunder Wolf, the old chief, had told the elders that it was the beginning of the end for the People.

In a short while the Sioux, the Arapaho, the Pawnee and the Apache, Comanche, and Kiowa were attacking the wagon trains. So the reports had said, and soon the soldiers had come.

Running Arrow had been at one of the first great peace meetings when, with a number of other tribes, they had "touched the pen," while a white man wrote down their names on the paper. Surely there was going to be peace.

Yet it seemed that nothing could bring peace. And it was soon as clear as the sun standing in the great sky that there would be no going back to the Shining Times.

Even so, there were old men who had spoken for peace with the white man. In spite of the sicknesses that the whites brought—the cholera, they called it, and then the sickness with the terrible spots, which killed thousands. And then came the killing of the buffalo, which was the worst. The peace chiefs, such as himself, Running Arrow, kept trying to live with the white man, for they wished more than anything to hold their people together. But it was a losing struggle.

All this and more was in Running Arrow's mind, and in his people too, as Clint Adams rode into the camp in the late forenoon. Clint felt it; he saw it in the stolid faces, whose very lack of expression told much more than words or gesture.

When he dismounted in front of the chief's lodge, there was a slight movement toward him among the onlookers. But at a word from the warriors who had escorted him in, the onlookers grew still; though for Clint, their anger was more tangible in the fresh silence.

The muttering started up again in the crowd, and some of the men pressed forward, heedless of the warnings of the escorting braves.

Clint had remained calm in the face of the growling and muttering and was considering saying something to the crowd, but at that point Running Arrow stepped out of his lodge; the muttering and gesticulating died down, leaving behind an atmosphere silent, yet vibrant with hostility.

"We will smoke first," the chief said. And he spoke in Sioux to one of his headmen.

A young brave then brought a blanket, and Running Arrow entered his lodge, signaling Clint to follow him. The blanket had been spread on the ground in front of the small fire, and now the chief sat down crosslegged, and Clint sat opposite him.

Carefully the pipe was prepared, offered to the Four Directions, to the Above and the Below, and then passed.

Running Arrow spoke. "I see that you bring news, Adams."

"I have found out who the men are—the wolfers who spread the poison."

"You followed them? You saw?" The chief looked directly at him, and it was as though the old warrior's eyes were piercing him.

"I followed them, and I saw them butcher a buffalo after shooting it. Then they gutted it and laid out poison. Then I followed them to just beyond the butte, the eastern side leading away from your camp. I can draw you a picture where the poison is. It is close to your camp."

"Not that close; my scouts would have seen them," the chief said.

"As I said, it is the other side of the butte, just off the reservation." When he had finished speaking, Clint reached into his shirt pocket and took out a piece of buffalo meat in which strychnine had been embedded. He handed it to Running Arrow, leaning up on his knees so that his hand and arm would not be scorched in the fire.

"I see that you respect our ways," the chief said suddenly. "You respect the fire."

"I didn't want to get burned," Clint said quietly.

"No, it was more than that."

"Yes." Clint nodded. "It was more than that." And then he said, "Thank you, Running Arrow. It is often easy to forget important things."

"I know."

They sat then for a while and presently talked about the poison and the men who had spread it. And Clint drew a map on the dirt floor of the lodge to show the places where the wolfers had placed the strychnine pellets.

"They did not see you or hear you?" Running Arrow asked.

"No. I would not be here talking with you if they had," Clint replied.

"I will send men to bring the poisoned meat before any bad thing happens," Running Arrow told him; and he called out.

Immediately, the same warrior who had brought the blanket entered. The chief conversed with him in Sioux, obviously giving instructions and making sure the young man understood.

As the Indian brave withdrew, Clint could feel that his attitude toward him had changed. He felt relieved.

"I will tell this to the agent man," Running Arrow said.

"And I will tell it to the army, or I might have to send someone."

"Is there not a lawman in the place you are? That village?"

"Willow Crossing?"

"I do not know the white-man name."

"There hadn't been a town marshal for a long while," Clint explained. "But now they have somebody at last."

"Then you could tell that man, too."

"Yes, I could. But it would not help us in any way."

The chief again had his eyes fully on him. "Why not tell? Is he a bad man, like so many others?"

"He is. Also he is two. He is two bad men."

"They have two lawmen now and not just one?"

Clint nodded. "They are twins."

"Twins?"

"Brothers, but exactly the same."

"So one does not know which brother is which one."

"That is so, plus they are not really with the law."

The chief just looked at him then.

"The two men are with the man of the wagon train that was attacked by Raven and Small Talker in the false way; when the guns were exchanged." Clint watched for a reaction.

The chief's eyes flashed at the mention of the guns. "So..."

A long silence fell then, and Clint knew the chief had to be thinking of the rifles and the difficulties they were going to bring upon his band.

Finally Running Arrow spoke. "We will smoke again," he said, "and I will tell you about the rifles and about Raven and Small Talker, who have been punished."

NINE

The shapely, ravishing redhead with the ostrich plume in her hat and a monkey on her arm created a good bit more than a ripple that afternoon on the Main Street of Willow Crossing. All she did was get off the Casper stage and walk half a block to the Frisco House, while the stage driver, old Leo Shivers, carried her trunk on his shoulder, moving along now as though he were ten years younger than sixty. Meanwhile, a couple of drunks and some mischievous boys fell in behind the lady and laughed when the monkey showed his displeasure by baring his teeth and made jungle sounds none of them had ever heard before. In only a moment the two drunks and the boys had grown into a crowd that pushed its way into the hotel lobby behind the lady and her monkey, practically breathing down her neck and into the tresses of her red hair, as she bent slightly to write her name in the hotel register.

Suddenly she turned on them, her beautiful features tight with annoyance. "I think you must go. I don't care for crowds, and therefore you may leave. Now!" And she stamped her foot. This movement, plus her crisp British accent and, even more, the authority with which she delivered her command, stunned the whole group. Even the drunks were silent. Although one, who had joined the crowd in the hotel lobby as he came downstairs from his room, peered at the hotel register and read aloud, "Constance Cuttlebone, Stoking-on-Thames." He was a lean man and his adam's apple was highly visible as it pumped up and down in his scrawny neck. "Holy Moses!" he declaimed. "Now whar in hell is Stoking Thames?"

The clerk, leaning forward onto his desk as the unwanted guests departed, raised his eyebrows as he read the name again. "Cuttlebone, is it? Well then, you got to be . . ." But the lady in question had turned on her heel and was instructing Leo, the stage driver, to put her trunk in her room.

"I am going for a walk. I need a breath of air."

When Leo had come back down to the hotel lobby the lady was gone, and an astonished room clerk, Carey McGovern, was scratching his head. "She has got to be the wife or daughter or sister or one thing or another of that English duke or lord or whichever the hell he was that was here not so damn long ago. Cuttle . . ."

He scratched his head, studied his fingernail to see what it was he'd rousted out, then brushed whatever it was away. "Bone. Cuttlebone. Jesus!" And reaching beneath the desk, he brought out a bottle and two glasses and offered refreshment to Leo, who, after carrying that heavy steamer trunk, was in sore need of the same.

Not very long after this startling first appearance in town, the lady in question, accompanied by her monkey, took the barflies in Miller's Tunnel Saloon completely by surprise by pushing her way through them to take a position behind a draw-poker player who was seriously considering laying down his hand in the face of a $400 raise.

The player facing this interesting predicament was Lucky Hands Harper, a man of wealth though questionable background, though he gave the appearance in not only demeanor but in speech of a man educated in the niceties of life. Yet he was famous for his associations with characters who were known to come from shifting backgrounds.

Lucky Hands had become instantly aware of someone standing behind him, and he turned in his chair to have a look. It was not accepted in a poker game to stand directly behind a player. Of course, there was nothing wrong in looking; after all, every poker game for high stakes pulled a gallery. One could look on from a respectable distance, but to crowd up close was to run right up against an unwritten law.

But what Lucky Hands saw evidently reassured him, for he said, "Boys, it looks like this is my lucky day. I'll call and raise five hundred."

The man he'd raised put down his cards. "I reckon

you could beat kings over jacks, Lucky. Looks like you win."

Lucky Hands pulled in the pot, then turned his cards face up on the table. He had queens over jacks.

The man Lucky had backwatered got up angrily from the table and stalked from the room.

Lucky Hands Harper stood up then, ready to speak to the lady standing behind his chair, but she had already turned and was walking out of the room, still holding her monkey on her arm.

"Well I'll be doggoned," muttered the famous gambler. "If that don't beat all!"

Clint Adams had witnessed the entire scene from only a short distance away. And he had heard the name Cuttlebone mentioned a couple of times. He leaned against the bar now, supported by his elbows, and studied the room. The woman had certainly made an impression that would not soon be forgotten. And it wasn't only the monkey but her own self; she didn't need any monkey. But what was she doing here in Willow Crossing?

He had heard about Cecil Cuttlebone. The gossip in town was full of the name. But there had been no mention of another Cuttlebone. Especially one of such beauty. He decided he would ask Hildebrand whether he knew anything more about Cuttlebone, not by any means to forget Mrs. Cuttlebone. His thoughts turned now to the knobby little man with the bald head and all those lines in his face.

It was Hildebrand who had taken the news of the poisoning to the army post at Fort Stanton, though he had returned with nothing in the way of a promise of help.

"Thing is," Hildebrand explained, "the army, like

everyone else, is overworked and undermanned. They're willing—the captain was—but he's bogged down with the usual shitload."

"I'll have to tell Running Arrow something," Clint said, and he felt a sinking inside him.

"Captain Harrigan did promise to send someone to investigate as soon as he could, but he didn't know for sure when. Seems there's been a little trouble with some Arapaho up around Wind Mountain." Hildebrand shrugged.

Clint asked if he'd questioned the captain about the Spencers. Hildebrand said Harrigan knew nothing about any Spencers. "At that point his interest had certainly increased. He said he would definitely look into it."

"And what about Running Arrow's band?" Clint asked. "Did you ask if the army was thinking of moving them again? The chief is really concerned about that."

Hildebrand said he had asked, and the captain had said there wasn't much chance of that, unless Washington changed its mind—which, Clint pointed out, was not the most unlikely thing to happen. Well, at least he had tried, and he could tell that to Running Arrow.

Clint knew, of course, as did the captain and Hildebrand, that the guns in question would have long since been very well hidden and the army wouldn't find even a trace of them. Clint knew Running Arrow would see to that, for the chief would not want to give up Raven and Small Talker to the white man's justice, no matter what they'd done. He was surely firm on that, as were the other chiefs he had known.

Now, as he quietly watched the action in the barroom, his thoughts turned to Stillox, who he knew had been going around town raising money for a new church. The reverend had also worked his way onto the town council and was attending meetings and holding out a glad hand to the useful—usable—citizens of Willow Crossing.

He had just ordered another beer when, looking into the mirror behind the bar, he saw the woman again. Cuttlebone! She came sweeping through the batwing doors, without the monkey this time, and bore directly down on one of the poker tables. In an instant, a charged atmosphere had gripped the room.

"Gentlemen," she said, standing before a group of astonished cardplayers, "I'd like to try my hand at a few rounds of poker. Is this a game that would accept a woman? An English woman?"

Someone found his voice and offered her a seat. It wasn't Lucky Hands Harper, who had already left the premises, obviously not realizing—as who, possibly, could have?—that the gorgeous redhead had only left in order to place her monkey somewhere. Who could have guessed at such a glorious return?

Clint Adams was delighted. He moved quickly toward the table where she had seated herself and where a crowd of eager onlookers had gathered; stunned and enchanted by such a marvelous diversion.

It was a colorful band that now made its way north of the Double Bar Cross toward the Wapiti Mountains. Some of the men were lean and silent, clad in faded buckskin, moccasins and fur caps; others were talkative, Frenchmen mostly, wearing dark blue hooded coats, crimson sashes, and a couple sported old-fashioned powder horns.

Of course, Riot McTeague had realized, on watching the unique retinue as it left the Double Bar, that they weren't going to find much to shoot at. Only some elk, antelope, some deer, and then smaller game—rabbits or coyotes; maybe prairie dogs. He knew that Seal Cuttlebone realized this; they had discussed it, along about their third bottle of wine. But no matter. For the gentleman had eventually informed the rancher that he was not really intent on hunting so much as he was on writing a book of his great adventures in the wild and woolly West. He had assured McTeague that he would be making a lot of money on this enterprise and so would pry himself quite out of the large amount of debt into which his wife had dug him.

"Connie is a spendthrift," he had told his host. "And she has been driving us to the poorhouse for years. Heedless for me to keep reminding the dear thing that the fact that she would be there with me did not in the least mitigate such dreadful circumstances." He had chuckled, jovial all the way through his rotund body.

He was the perfect tool, McTeague told himself. Not a man in Willow Crossing believed his story of hunting for big game. Hell, there wasn't any! How many times did it have to be said! So what was an English lord, duke, or whatever, doing out here with all these followers, all that booze, and obviously, money? *Obviously!* It was as plain as a dive off a mad-as-hell bronc that the man had to be after something else!

Both he and Thorpe McCool had seen him as the

perfect card for their play. All the better, since Cuttlebone had no notion at all that he was being used. The man—or, rather, his agent—had simply approached the Liverpool Company asking for information about the American West, about hunting, and had run into Thorpe, who, in a flash had realized an opportunity to expand his company's holdings up around Stud Basin. Of course, Thorpe had realized the need to work in cooperation with McTeague and his Double Bar Cross outfit. McTeague, for his part, had seen McCool as a useful partner. Each had recognized the very obvious fact that the relationship between them was only going to be of a certain duration. But nothing of this was ever spoken. It was simply a fact. There. Each would make use of the other as he could. McCool, an elegant operator with connections in the East and, of course, in Liverpool, England, saw Riot McTeague as a pawn in the game. McTeague, meanwhile, saw McCool and his company as something usable. And eventually disposable. Hence the wolfers. The owner of all that real estate in Willow Crossing and all that range land bordering on Stud Basin and the Sioux reservation hadn't told anyone how he was increasing his small cadre of wolfers, who by now numbered almost two dozen. Only L. T. Moses knew this for sure. L. T. didn't like it, but that was of no consequence to his boss. As L. T. realized full well, a man who could dig a grave with an enemy and then fight him to the death in it was not a man to argue with unnecessarily.

Meanwhile, the Cuttlebone party worked its way north toward the Wapitis, guided by the fabled scout, hunter, trapper, frontiersman, and prospector Paris Tbalt.

Not too far behind the party, McTeague and his wolfers now followed. McTeague wanted to be sure of two things: the direction Cuttlebone was taking, and, at the same time, he wanted to know the caliber of his own little army of wolfers.

Thus far, he was working openly with Thorpe McCool, with the understanding that at a certain point he would contact Paris, whose penchant for larceny he'd known from way back.

It would be then, at that particular point, that the lid would blow. It would be up to Paris to do it right, but McTeague had confidence in the man—that is, as much as he ever allowed himself to trust anyone other than himself. But it was at that point, too, that he would have to move into his own plan regarding the big parcel of land—the very big parcel of land— known as Stud Basin.

And so, after following the Cuttlebone party for a day and a half, and observing the quality of his wolfers, he had turned them over to L. T. Moses and ridden back to the Double Bar. It was necessary now to get in touch with Fancy Joe Stillox and see to those Spencers and the Spencer ammo.

Yes, he was on his way. He grinned at the thought. Hell, the town, the outfit, it had all been fun, but it was small stuff. This, now, was big. Real big. Empire. He liked the sound of the word. By God, the plan—his plan—was big. And that was a gut!

At the Tunnel Saloon the betting was brisk at the corner table where the beautiful redhead had seated herself and was now dealing, with a king showing on the second round. The man seated across from her had an ace exposed. He bet $400. All the other players dropped out, and when it was the lady's turn to bet she called and raised $400.

The gambler she was facing was a man Clint Adams had seen before, in a Denver gambling hall. His name was Phil Dappleby. Clint knew he was a veteran graduate of the Mississippi River gambling boats. A tall, pale man with a chiseled nose and mouth and a delicate jaw, Clint figured him for a sly customer who likely used advantage tools. Yet the Gunsmith had a feeling that the lady dealing those cards had something that could equal anything a man like Phil Dappleby could throw at her.

Now Dappleby said, "I don't like to take advantage of a woman, but I'll have to tap you. I have a pair of aces, and your kings can't beat me unless you catch another. How much have you there?"

Constance Cuttlebone counted out her chips, worth $1,000. Dappleby matched them. "All right then. Deal 'em," he said. And he turned his hole ace over to show that he was honest.

The lady dealt the rest of the cards, and on the fifth round she caught a third king. All Dappleby could come up with was a pair of aces.

She reached for the pot, but Dappleby stopped her. "Just a minute. That third king was deep in the deck. I saw it flash when you riffled the cards, and I cut light."

"So you cut light. You were taking an advantage in cutting light, and the king wasn't where you thought it was." And she drew in the pot.

Clint had been watching the play closely. He had seen nothing wrong with the deal, nor, he realized, had any of the other onlookers. Neither had Dappleby seen anything funny about the deal, except it was obvious to the Gunsmith that he had buried the king. Clint knew that since there were four kings in the deck, and three had landed in Constance Cuttlebone's hand, there was every reason to suppose that the fourth king had popped up.

Dappleby demanded to examine the deck, and the lady handed it over with a smile. The fourth king was three cards from the bottom.

"That proves you slipped yourself the third king!" Dappleby declared angrily, but the onlookers and players hooted him down, and finally he got to his feet and left the place. The man had accused a woman of cheating, and the onlookers didn't like it. Even if she had cheated, Dappleby could prove nothing, Clint knew; and he had, of course, left himself wide open by admitting that he had tried to bury the king so it wouldn't crop up, thus proving his own dishonesty.

The lady stood the drinks but appeared not to want anything for herself. Her companions from the poker game—minus Dappleby—lined up at the bar for the drink she was buying them, and Clint saw his chance.

"There's an empty table over in that corner," he said, moving quickly to her side. "Would you join me? They happen to have some really good champagne just in from San Francisco."

She turned to face him, surprise in her face, and then she laughed. "Ah, yes, the careful watcher standing behind that rather stout gentleman. I was wondering when you were going to ask me." And without waiting for Clint to reply, she started in the direction of the table he had indicated.

Delighted at her swift realization of the situation, he quickly ordered the champagne and reached the table just as she was seating herself.

"I'm Clint Adams," he said.

"I am Constance Cuttlebone."

"I know," he said, as the bartender appeared with a cold bottle and two cold glasses. Clint had assumed McTeague would have such items as champagne on hand and in the necessary condition, and he had told the bartender accordingly, with the appropriate amount of persuasion.

The pop of the cork caused heads to turn—not that they weren't under surveillance already—but both ignored the rest of the barroom.

"What do you do for a living, Mr. Adams?"

"Clint. I'm a gunsmith. I repair guns and also rebuild them. I have a team and wagon and I travel about, getting work here and there."

"I see." She was smiling at him over the rim of her raised glass of champagne.

Together they drank a silent toast.

She was still smiling at him as he said, "And you? Are you Miss or Mrs.?"

"Not Miss." And she took another sip of champagne. "It's really topnotch."

"I see, Mrs., then."

Her eyes did not leave his face as she said, "Sometimes." And before he could say anything to that, she had raised her glass again and drained it.

"Thank you, sir."

She stood up, and his eyes took in the swelling of her perfectly rounded breasts, the firm, prominent nipples of which her green satin blouse did nothing to hide.

"Goodnight, Mr. Adams," she said, and her voice was louder than it had been. "Thank you for your hospitality." Then, turning toward some of the faces that had been watching the scene, she said, "And for yours, gentlemen."

And she swept out of the room, the way opening for her as before royalty.

Clint had another glass of champagne quietly, waiting for a suitable length of time to pass. He was just finishing his glass when Oleander Hildebrand appeared.

"That looks like good stuff," he said, eyeing the bottle. "I hear that Cuttlebone's missus was here, making quite a stir."

"That she did," Clint said with a grin. "Get yourself a glass." Then he saw that Hildebrand already had a glass in his hand.

"Figured you'd ask me," he said, pretending to look sheepish. "You got time to talk?"

"I've got time to hear your news," the Gunsmith said.

"Still sharp, ain't you," Hildebrand said pleasantly as he poured himself a drink. "Well, you were right about the wolfers. I just got back in town. McTeague's got a whole mess of those boys out at the Double Bar Cross. And his lordship is heading toward the Wichita range to see what he can get in the way of trophies."

"But by way of Stud Butte," said Clint, raising his eyebrows as though to verify what he'd said.

Hildebrand nodded. "You're figuring that's where the action is then?"

"It's Indian country all around there, and the boundary isn't any too clear. But think of those

Spencers. Even if they don't have a whole helluva lot of ammo, just the knowing that they've got 'em will scare the shit out of half the country."

Hildebrand had been nodding as he'd said this. "And that'll be the end of Running Arrow and his band, likely," he said.

"Somebody wants them off that land," Clint said.

"Somebody?" Hildebrand cocked his head sagely at his companion. "Could I guess who?" he asked, with a droll expression on his wrinkled face. "Like a man with initials like, uh, Riot McTeague?"

"Not too sure yet," Clint said thoughtfully. "It's a real big ringy-doo, that one. I figure Riot has got to have help somewhere."

Suddenly all those wrinkles seemed to open on Oleander Hildebrand's face. "Like you mean his lordship Mr. Cuttlepants?"

But Clint Adams shook his head. "He could be part of it; maybe. But I don't think he's the moneybags. I mean, let's look at it. McTeague and those wolfers can only go so far. They're more like backup. They're not in any way an army. What I'm saying is, where's McTeague getting his punch from?"

Hildebrand nodded. "I see what you mean. McTeague is big, he's tough, but he ain't that big." He scratched into his beard. "I got two things," he said, lowering his voice considerably.

"What have you got?" Clint asked, also lowering his voice. "A railroad? Cattle company? Landgrabbers who want to 'develop,' as they put it?"

"One is Cuttlebone. He's as fake as a five-ace pack of cards."

"But the question is, who is he fake for?" said

Clint. "And while we're at it, what about Stillox?"

"I've seen him with McTeague."

"So have I."

Hildebrand took out his tobacco sack and papers and thoughtfully built himself a smoke. "The reason isn't so important, the way I look at it. It don't matter whether it's the railroad or sodbusters getting sold land with hardly any topsoil, or whether it's simply for the stockgrowers."

"Aren't you one of their detectives?" Clint asked. "Or is it Wells, Fargo?"

"I have been both and each in my time," Hildebrand said. "Right now I have been investigating for the Cheyenne Cattlemen's Association. Not that I'm in favor of those big boys, Adams. I know your views—I think—on those matters. But a living's a living. Mostly, though, I'm trying to find who killed my friend Mitch Durham. Been wondering if the killing was ordered."

"Ordered?" Clint leaned back in his wooden round-back chair. Then he leaned forward again, with his elbows on the table, his eyes on the man across from him.

"Mitch was investigating the Liverpool Cattle Company's connections in Wyoming, especially a man named McCool. Thorpe McCool. Ever hear of him?"

"Do you know if he got too close? Is that it?"

"Could be. But I could be climbing the wrong tree."

"Liverpool, I have heard, has grabbed up a lot of territory," Clint said, reaching for his tobacco and papers but then deciding to light a quirly instead. "You still haven't spoken with Molly Durham?"

Hildebrand shook his head. "But maybe it's time. She might know something she doesn't know she knows."

"I was thinking just that," Clint said.

He pushed back his chair and stood up. "So long."

"Good luck," Oleander Hildebrand said, and Clint saw that his face was as bland as any of those pies he must have bitten into during his championship days.

Only minutes later, he was at the Frisco House front door. Looking through the glass, he saw that the clerk was snoozing behind his desk. He didn't hesitate but walked right in.

When he knocked on the desktop, the clerk awoke with a start. He was a young boy, and he had a lot of freckles all over his face. He couldn't have been more than fourteen.

"You the room clerk?"

"Yes sir. That is, the regular, Mr. Saul, he took sick and my uncle Theo ast me to do it."

"You have a message for Clint Adams?"

"Lemme look." He turned to the small table behind him and picked up a piece of paper, as an envelope slipped to the floor.

"That there looks like it," Clint said, pointing to the envelope.

"You got good eyesight, mister," the boy said, as Clint slit open the envelope and read what was inside.

He looked up at the boy now, slipping the note into his pocket. The boy was chewing on a stick of licorice.

"Give me my key there, will you. Number seven."

The boy knew his job. He handed over the key

and checked it against the ledger on the desk.

"Good night," he said, as he watched Clint start toward the stairs. "If you need anything, Mr. Adams, just holler."

Clint realized the boy had heard of the Gunsmith: It was in his tone of voice, in his words, in his offer of assistance.

"I don't figure on needing anything," Clint said as he climbed the stairs.

But whether the boy heard him or not, he didn't know; nor did he care.

TEN

The lady's legs were superb. Indeed, her entire anatomy left nothing that needed to be imagined. It was all there—to see, to touch, to enjoy.

Clint Adams not only reveled in the sight of her—the touch, her odor—but even more in what she did with what she had in such delightful amounts.

He had knocked discreetly at her door and it had opened almost immediately. Without a word being said they embraced, his lips melting hungrily into hers, his rigid organ thrusting between her parted legs.

"I've been dying with impatience," she said as he removed her clothing.

"The same here, but I thought it better not to follow you too soon."

"Teaser!" she whispered into his ear. She reached

down between his legs. "Oh, I knew you had a big one!" And with a quiver running all through her body, she lay back on the bed and spread her legs, still holding his penis.

She was soaking, her come all through her great mass of pubic hair, as she guided his erection in.

As their loins slid into their dance, Clint thought he had seldom met such an agreeable partner. They moved quietly, gently, taking long, slow strokes, then building up slowly as their rhythm increased and he probed her deeper and higher. Now she began to breathe heavily, and a gasp broke from her as he drove deeper into her. Finally they were moving totally as one body, each anticipating the other's move and bringing it to its impossibly delightful climax. And they lay gasping together as they came in great waves and little oceans of exquisite pleasure.

After they had finished, he lay on top of her for a long while, his body almost embedded in hers, until his penis had softened completely, yet he kept it inside. He started to withdraw, but she grabbed him with her arms and legs and whispered, "No!"

And at that his erection grew again until it was just as hard as before, and they were moving, dancing their sex dance together, their thighs slithering with the come that poured down her thighs as she moved in perfect unison with him, and they built that rhythm to a perfect climax.

Again they lay still locked together, with him on top of her. Then, after some moments, he rolled off and now lay next to her.

Finally she spoke. "I had heard of the Western hospitality being rather exceptional, Mr. Adams, but

I must confess I'd no idea how wonderfully exceptional it was."

"Just wanted you to feel welcome, ma'am," he said, with a hayseed tone of voice.

She giggled then. "You're a real good lay, buddy," she said.

"Likewise."

"By the way, have you by any chance met my husband? I mean, actually, would you happen to know where he is?"

"I believe he's somewhere up around the Wapiti Mountains, with his retainers, his guns, his knives, and all his food and liquor and servants."

"Hunting?"

"Hunting. No, I've never met him, though I have heard about him. Do you plan to join him?"

"I had come out for that purpose, plus the grim fact that I do need money. But no, mostly because I was getting bored back in New York." And she raised herself suddenly on one elbow, with one of her breasts bouncing right into his face.

Reaching up, he took it by its nipple and guided it to his mouth. She leaned down, sighing, as he sucked and fluttered his tongue on its tender hardness.

"I want you this time," she said, climbing on top of him, and sitting down right on his erect peg, and wiggling her bottom.

The Gunsmith was not at all running out of ammunition, but still he had had two shots at the lady, and this time, though equally as good as the first two, was so excruciatingly sweet that as he felt the squirting of her come he could no longer delay his own ejaculation for that extra pleasure, and he came right then, totally with her. He knew, as she did, too, that the old adage was still true: The best one is the last one.

It was late afternoon in the Inside Straight Saloon & Gaming Parlor & Dance Palace and the boys were addressing themselves diligently to what was at hand —booze, cards, dice and other gambling activities, dull conversation, and, for more than a few, lurid dreams. Chrome stood with his arms extended in a v-shape as he leaned his palms on the bar from the sober side, eyeing his customers with his customary disdain. Chrome did not approve of excessive drinking, though he was a fairly noble imbiber himself— an anomaly in character with which many citizens in Willow Crossing could live. There were even some who disapproved of illicit copulation while not infrequently visiting the girls in the cribs.

The Twin Buttes, now marshals of the town, were of this split persuasion: disapproving of certain functions in which they themselves indulged. Emphatically, their disapproval was invariably reserved for others. Thus the twins from time to time would descend on some hapless drinker or fornicator and threaten or even actually execute law enforcement on same: a night in prison or the threat of exposure to a gentleman's family. On the other hand, threats toward one of the cyprians who was only trying to earn a dollar the easy way could—and in fact generally did—turn into a simple exchange in trade, an example of efficient barter. The twin in question would receive the pleasure of the lady in question for not enforcing "the law"; in the case of liquor, free drinks were the salve that eased the wounded feelings caused by seeing wanton indulgence in grain or grape.

At the moment, the twins had just entered the Inside Straight, and Chrome, along with One-Eye Gallagher had spotted them in the same split second. Pretty hard not to.

"Like a whiskey here," Clancy said. And Nole nodded in agreement.

Nole now turned around with his back to the bar and surveyed the crowded room. "Heared you got coupla new girls, Chrome," he said out of the side of his mouth.

Chrome knew what was coming. "Just started one last night," he said.

"She brought in money yet?" Clancy asked.

Chrome said, "You'd have to ask One-Eye on that one. He handles that part of the establishment." Chrome did not at all care for the twins, especially since they were newcomers to Willow Crossing, but he was a man who knew how to keep his mouth shut, and his skin attached to his body.

"Goosey," Nole said to his brother as they reached for their free drinks. "I am feelin' real goosey, Brother."

"Likewise."

"What say we take on a couple of them new girls?"

"Or why not the one," Clancy said, grinning at his brother. "Like that one over to Gallon City that time had us both at the same time."

His brother joined his grin at that remark, remembering the ruckus they'd had.

Suddenly Nole felt his brother stiffen beside him. "Watcha got, Clance?" he asked, speaking low and inching his hand closer to the six-gun that rode prominently at his hip.

"Look at that son-of-a-bitch," said Clancy, his words hard and cold as ice. He was staring into the mirror in back of the bar.

His brother had not moved, remaining in the same position he'd been in so as not to excite any unnecessary comment.

"Sounds like you seen the same son-of-a-bitch we had trouble with before," Nole said.

"It is him."

Nole raised his eyes to the mirror now, and they both slowly turned as Clint Adams moved through the room.

"We gonna call him?" Nole asked.

"Too crowded. But we could set it up outside."

But there was no conviction in the words of either of them. Seeing the Gunsmith look over in their direction, both dropped their eyes and pretended to be in conversation.

Clint had spotted the Twin Buttes the moment he'd walked in. Actually, he'd been looking for Oleander Hildebrand, but the gentleman was not there.

He was just deciding whether or not to hang around on the chance that Hildebrand might show up when, to his own astonishment as well as everyone else's in the room, an incredible figure pushed through the swinging doors of the saloon. It was a moment before the rest of the clientele saw him, but they did; save those, of course, who had their heads, hands, noses, and thoughts buried in poker, dice, the wheel of fortune, or faro. Even with so many interested in gaming, there were still quite a few left over who stared incredulously at the brilliantly bedraggled figure of Paris Tbalt, all hair and buckskin and clearly the worse—or maybe the better—for wear from a clear overdose of booze.

"Hey, Paris, where's your duke? You quit him, or you got your ass busted?" someone called out.

"Go fuck yerself!" shouted the old scout to the anonymous joker. "I got mine, by God, and I ain't workin' my ass off for no jackass English dude, by God!"

At which point somebody deliberately—or maybe accidentally—stuck out his foot, and, to the delight of the onlookers, Paris took a spill, crashing to the floor.

But the old boy, spry as a spring chicken, was up on his feet in a jiffy, boxing his fists in front of him at an imaginary opponent. "C'mon, you bugger! You trip me, I'm gonna wipe the floor with ye, by jingo!" And he danced around the space that had suddenly cleared for him, boxing at his imagined foe, until finally he swung too hard and was carried off his feet. This time as he landed something fell from his pocket—or seemed to: There was speculation later as to whether the object had really fallen when he'd first tripped. It didn't matter, for as the shout went up—and following a split second of astounded silence—the barroom turned into bedlam. And the word "Gold!" rang through the room, hitting walls, charging out into the street, and in only moments it was all over town. For what had dropped from Paris Tbalt's pocket was a packet of yellow dust. And it was only minutes before the word was everywhere, and everybody knew why Sir Cecil Cuttlebone had gone hunting for game that wasn't there. Everyone knew—thanks to Paris Tbalt's unfortunate "accident"—that Sir Cecil Cuttlebone wasn't anywhere near as dumb as he'd been taken for.

Gold!

During the next several moments following Paris Tbalt's mishap, the Gunsmith remained standing just where he was. He kept his eyes on the old scout, who was up on his feet again and arguing with the men around him: that it was all a mistake; that the bit of dust was nothing, only something he'd had with him all along; that there was no gold strike and not even a chance of one.

But the more he argued and tried to persuade them, the less they believed him; indeed, in only a short while the wiser ones gave up trying to get the location of the strike out of the reluctant old scout and simply ran off to get ready for the ride out to the Wapiti country, where it was known that Cuttlebone and his party had been headed.

In a short while the saloon was deserted, save for Clint Adams and Paris, who had stepped briskly behind the unattended bar to pour himself some liquid support for the ragging, bedeviling, and even pummeling he had received.

A silence now fell over the room as the two men watched each other amidst the overturned tables and chairs, the broken bottles and glassware.

"Not going goldhunting, Mr. Gunsmith?" the old scout, trapper, frontiersman, and spinner of tall tales asked.

"Paris, you should have been an actor."

"Dunno what you mean, sir."

"There is about as much gold out yonder where all those damn fools are running as there is salt water."

WAGON TRAIN TO HELL 173

Clint put down his drink and walked over to the old man who was sitting on top of the bar, holding a tumbler of whiskey in his hand and sucking his teeth.

"Who put you up to it, Paris? Cuttlebone? McTeague?"

"Dunno what you're talkin' about, Gunsmith. I reckon you have gone plumb loco. I tolt them buzzards there wasn't no gold!"

It was at that moment that Oleander Hildebrand walked into the Inside Straight and surveyed the charged tableau—the wrecked saloon, the old scout, and the grim Clint Adams bracing him.

"I want answers, Paris. I mean right now!"

"You gonna shoot me, Gunsmith, if I just keep tellin' you the truth?"

"I asked you a question." Clint turned toward Hildebrand, who had come up beside him. "I reckon you have figured it out, Oleander."

"That I have." He looked at the old scout, who was just beginning to have some doubts as he faced not just one but two determined and heavily armed men.

It was in the next second that Clint realized he might have miscalculated, for he saw something come into Paris Tbalt's eyes. He wouldn't have been able to give it a name; nevertheless, it was there. And out of the corner of his eye, in the big mirror, he saw the movement at the back of the room.

"Gunsmith!"

And Clint dropped onto his back, rolled, drew his Colt, and fired one shot lying down, followed by a second shot as he was half raised on his elbow.

His first shot caught Nole in the throat; his second drilled his brother, Clancy, right through the heart.

"God almighty!" Those holy words broke from Hildebrand, who hadn't even drawn his gun before the twins were down.

"Jesus Jehosephat!" said Paris Tbalt. "By God, yours truly has seen it all!" His eyes were bugging out of his head as they looked at the twin bodies on the floor.

Suddenly he remembered something, and he straightened up, fast, like a soldier coming to attention. "You wuz axin' me a question there, Mr. Adams, sir. But would you mind tellin' it again? I sure as hell do want to answer it!"

"Hildebrand, you and Tbalt here had better ride out fast to Running Arrow's camp."

Hildebrand, still in slight shock from the scene he had witnessed, nodded. "You figger all those crazy goldhunters are gonna go busting through there and start a war?"

"That's the idea of whoever planned this thing. Then the army comes in, takes over and moves the Sioux, and the land is up for the man with his offer in his hand."

"Liverpool."

"And Riot McTeague."

"Sure enough."

"Take the fastest horses you can get down at the livery. And you!" He wheeled on Paris Tbalt, but the old boy stood his ground even so. He was chewing his tobacco real fast.

"Gunsmith—I mean, Mr. Adams—this is a real shit-pisser, but Paris Tbalt is with you!"

"You won't be changing sides again?" Hildebrand asked.

"Nozzah! Not goin' agin a man who shoots so fast his second bullet overtakes his first!"

Suddenly a groan reached them, and they realized that one of the twins was still alive.

"I could get a doc," Hildebrand said, as they stood looking down at the twin who had been shot through the throat.

"Too late," Clint said, as the man finally did die.

"Hell," said Hildebrand. "I was hoping he'd tell who shot Mitch. I figure it could be one of them."

Clint said nothing, and both men turned to him. He was standing very still, as though listening.

"What?" Hildebrand asked, speaking softly and with his hand on his holstered six-gun.

"Thought I heard something. But it's gone. You better get going. After you see Running Arrow, head for Fort Stanton."

"And you?"

"I'll stay here. I've a notion McTeague will be coming in sooner or later." He had been reloading the Colt while he was talking, and now he slipped it back into its holster. "You men had better get going. Otherwise it won't be worth going at all. Hurry it, now. McTeague will have his wolfers all over the place out there at Stud Butte. Once the Sioux start on the path, they'll be butchered. I suppose they could use those Spencers as clubs, since they've got no ammo."

When they were gone, he walked over to the bar and poured himself a drink. He had just lifted his glass to take a swallow when he heard it again; the creak of a stair was what it sounded like. Yet he wasn't sure. It could be the wind, though there wasn't much wind about.

With his eyes watching the room through the mirror in back of the bar, Clint walked across to the stairs that led to the balcony and the girls' rooms. The building was silent now, and he could hear only an occasional shout in the street. He hoped that Hildebrand and Paris Tbalt were really cutting leather.

The feeling that he was not alone in the Inside Straight was growing within him. And the picture of Riot McTeague was in the front of his mind. By now, Clint was sure someone would have wondered where the Twin Buttes were and would soon come looking. There they lay in the middle of the barroom floor, almost as though they'd been laid out, for both were on their backs.

Then he heard the swinging doors creak open fast, and in walked Joseph Stillox.

"My God, what has happened!" He stood stock still, staring in disbelief at the two corpses.

"Somebody's plan went wrong, looks like," Clint said smoothly.

"My boys!" Stillox wasn't acting. His eyes bugged, and he began to sweat. He looked as if he were about to go down on his knees, but he held himself erect and removed his big Texas hat.

"Who shot them, Adams?"

"I did."

"I see."

Stillox was holding his hat in his hands, and the Gunsmith said, "Don't try it, Stillox. Unless you want to make it a threesome."

"I don't know what you mean, Adams!"

"Put your right hand down at your side; that's what I mean!"

"But..."

"He means he doesn't want you to interfere with me outgunning the son-of-a-bitch," said a hard voice coming from the balcony just above him. "Don't move, Gunsmith!" And Riot McTeague's wild laugh cracked through the beleaguered barroom.

"Joseph, I am going to settle something with this jackanapes. He thinks he is the fastest gun in the whole world, exceptin' he ain't gone up against Riot McTeague! Not yet! Gunsmith, I am challenging you!"

"Do you want to face me, McTeague, or are you going to put it in my back?"

"I am going to face you, you smart son-of-a-bitch. Turn around!"

Clint saw it now. If he turned to face McTeague, Stillox would shoot him in the back; and if he didn't, McTeague would do it. What was more, Stillox wouldn't have to draw, since he obviously had his gun in the crown of his hat, which he was holding in his hands.

Clint remained facing Stillox, trying to feel the room, watching his breath, listening to the intensity of the moment and himself in it. Never had he been so sensitized as at that next moment when a shot rang out—he wasn't sure from where—and he dropped as he had before with the twins and shot McTeague in his gun arm. Rolling, he came up to face Stillox, only to see the man lying on the floor, breathing his last. And there was Oleander Hildebrand, holstering his gun

"I had a notion, Adams, and I just had to follow it. Lucky I did."

"And Tbalt?"

"Paris is on his way to the Sioux and Fort Stanton."

But McTeague, who had screamed with rage and the pain of his right forearm being shattered, was now trying to pick up his gun with his left hand.

"Leave it!" snapped Clint. "And don't get the idea I missed killing you. I want you alive to spill your story to the army at Fort Stanton."

"You lousy son-of-a-bitch, Adams!"

"I'll go get a doc for him," Hildebrand said. You'll want him patched up so's he can give evidence."

Clint Adams almost missed it, but that extra sense that he invariably relied on had not deserted him. It was awfully close, and if he hadn't been experiencing that special sensitivity, he wouldn't have made it.

"Why don't you just shoot the bastard, Ollie, and be done with it!" said Riot McTeague, and he dove for his gun with his left hand.

Clint himself hardly knew how he moved, but he shot McTeague through his left arm this time; and before the twice-wounded man had time to scream at this fresh pain and frustration, the Gunsmith had twisted and, shooting from a bent-over position, his gun hand almost touching the floor, he drilled Oleander Hildebrand right in the middle of his chest.

Standing over the fallen man, Clint said, "You see what kind of a friend you've got there, Ollie. The rat figured he'd use you so he could get me."

Hildebrand was hardly able to breathe. He was gurgling as he managed the words. "When did you figure it, Gu...Gun..." But he couldn't get the word out, and he lay there with his eyes wide, pumping short, dying breaths.

"You didn't even leave for Fort Stanton or the Sioux camp. I could hear it in your voice. And hell, before that, well, I happen to know that Upper Sandusky isn't in Indiana but in Ohio. I didn't catch it at the time you said it, but just now it all clicked. It was you who killed Mitch Durham, wasn't it?"

By now Riot McTeague had stopped cursing. He turned toward the prone Hildebrand. "You stupid bastard!"

But Ollie Hildebrand was dead.

"He killed Durham when Durham got too close to your boys—that right, McTeague?"

"Soon as my arms mend I'll be coming for you, Adams."

"No you won't, mister. You know why? Because by the time you get out of the penitentiary, if somebody hasn't fitted you first with a vigilante collar, you'll be too damn old to pull a trigger."

Then, holstering his Colt after having reloaded it, he walked out of the Inside Straight Saloon + Gaming Parlor + Dance Palace.

It was just getting to be dawn. The air was fresh, yet he suddenly felt tired. He was sorry about Oleander Hildebrand; he had kind of liked the man in a certain way.

Later in the day the men who had gone racing out of town looking for gold began to straggle back. Most of them wore a sheepish look, but no one dared make fun of them.

Clint had sent someone to help McTeague get to the doctor. And through the grapevine he heard that

Sir Cecil Cuttlebone had shot a goodly amount of game. And it began to appear to him that the Englishman had no notion that he had been used by Riot McTeague, who wanted to build an empire, and by Thorpe McCool and the Liverpool outfit, who wanted to build an even bigger one.

Later that same day, he went to visit McTeague, who had been patched up by Doc Morse and now had his arms in splints and had to be fed by his redheaded girlfriend. The rancher was lying in bed at a friend's house, and he regarded his visitor sourly.

"I am not a lawman, McTeague, but I will be sending in a report to the army, so that Running Arrow's band will not be bothered about those Spencers you tried to hook them with."

"I don't care what you do. You can't stick me with anything. You can't prove anything."

"It's not my business to try," Clint said. "I'm not going to push anything. So long as you keep away from Sioux land. I want to hear your word on it."

"Sure, sure; here's my word!" And, trying to move his arm to make an obscene gesture, he became transfixed with pain and started to curse.

"I don't hold grudges," Clint said. "But I will urge the army to keep an eye on you and see that you don't mess with Running Arrow's people."

"Injun lover." The words came out, but there was no force in them.

"Glad to hear you agree with me," Clint said.

"I didn't agree with you, mister."

"Yes you did."

"No I didn't."

"Yes you did. I heard you."

"No I did not!"

"You did."

"Didn't!"

"Did."

"I did not."

"Did," said the Gunsmith, and he walked to the open door. "I heard it in your voice. You just don't want to admit it, you old fart!"

"Didn't," muttered the bandaged figure lying on the bed.

"If you think that man is going to say he did, Adams, you got another thing comin'," said L. T. Moses, now coming into view down the hall. "I heared the two of you all the way down the corridor, fer Christ sake!"

"And if you think yours truly is going to say he didn't, then you have got a mighty big thing coming," the Gunsmith said firmly, his lips tight and his eyes hard.

"Reckon I'll have to settle 'er then," said L. T. "Being as you two boys are gonna wear yerselves and all the rest of us down to our ankle bones."

"You settle it!" roared the man in bed. "Moses, I have always said that you by God damnit let that name of yours run off with your good sense, what little of same you do happen to have—sometimes," he added.

"Then listen to this," the foreman said. "You might not say you did, but we done did; the boys and myself. We agree with Adams, here. And before you start getting another hard-on there, God damnit, I have let all them stinkin' wolfers go, on account of you were gonna lose the whole of your hands who can't stand the stink of those shitpots. Including meself!"

"Is that the tablets, eh, Moses? You are trying to backwater me, huh!"

"Wouldn't think of such a thing, boss," L. T. said, swift as a wink and soft as a pussy cat. "We are all with you, man and boy." His carved face was as sweet as a choir singer's.

"You buggers think you got me by the balls," said the man on the bed.

"That ain't our line of work," said L. T. Moses, serious as a tombstone.

And, to the Gunsmith's astonishment, a grin started to appear on the McTeague face, which he swiftly smothered.

"When I get outta this here," McTeague said, grave again, "I am gonna show you half-assed cowhands how to bust a bronc or two. Shit, the way you got Stringer Jack and his buddy working that buckskin and them others, you wouldn't get a one of 'em to roping into a roundup herd! Now, somebody get me a drink!" He made a face as he tried to move one of his arms. "Shit! Somebody go get Angie so's she can help me drink."

"Angie's gonna have to help you do a whole lot of things, Mr. McTeague," L. T. said. "Now, don't get excited! I am talkin' about eating and drinking like."

McTeague sniffed. "Adams, I can tell you to be a stomper from the old days. You might like to draw some pay working for the Double Bar Cross. I need a good man to keep a eye on this half-assed ramrod I got here."

"I'll pass that one up, McTeague. But I will take that drink you offered."

"Damnit, I never offered you a drink!"

"Yes you did."

"No I didn't. You're crazy."

"You did," the Gunsmith said with maddening calmness.

"No."

"Yes."

"Holy Moses!" said L. T. Moses. "I am gonna have myself a whole bottle of the booze!"

By the time Angie had hustled into the room with a bottle of whiskey and some glasses, she found the three men waiting in stiff silence.

There was nothing for her to do but get another glass and join them.

The Gunsmith, a man who practically never had any difficulty making up his mind about anything, was indeed finding it difficult to come to a decision.

The indecision in question didn't bother him at all, really. In fact, he enjoyed it. The only thing to be careful about was not to fall into the old one about the donkey who starved to death standing between two bales of hay, unable to make up his mind. Certainly, Molly Durham and Connie Cuttlebone had not the slightest resemblance to a bale of hay. Yet the principle was there. Which one?

Each was a total delight.

Toward evening, he lay on his bed in the Frisco House, pondering the choice that had to be made, when suddenly he heard the step in the corridor outside, followed by a knock at his door.

He opened it, to find Connie Cuttlebone standing there. As he stepped back to let her in she handed him an envelope.

"The room clerk asked me to give this to you. It's very important, he said."

Clint slipped the envelope into his pocket.

"Aren't you going to open it?" she asked. "He said the person who delivered it said it was very important."

"Later," Clint said, as he began unbuttoning the long line of white buttons that ran the length of her dress.

He knew who the note was from. And he was glad it was working out this way. Things always did work out, one way or another.

He was very happy to have Connie first, for she was a true fleshy delight, and she brought him to the acme of ecstasy.

And when it was night, and she had left him, he read the note and then made his way to Molly Durham's rooming house, where they'd made love the last time. He was really looking forward to it. And he wasn't disappointed.

Even as a small boy, he'd always liked saving the best things for last.

Watch for

RIDE FOR REVENGE

*100th novel in the exciting
GUNSMITH series*

coming in April!

J.R. ROBERTS
THE
GUNSMITH

___ THE GUNSMITH #87: RIDE FOR VENGEANCE	0-515-09961-9/$2.95
___ THE GUNSMITH #88: THE TAKERSVILLE SHOOT	0-515-09987-2/$2.95
___ THE GUNSMITH #89: BLOOD ON THE LAND	0-515-10017-X/$2.95
___ THE GUNSMITH #90: SIXGUN SIDESHOW	0-515-10037-4/$2.95
___ THE GUNSMITH #91: MISSISSIPPI MASSACRE	0-515-10063-3/$2.95
___ THE GUNSMITH #92: THE ARIZONA TRIANGLE	0-515-10109-5/$2.95
___ THE GUNSMITH #93: BROTHERS OF THE GUN	0-515-10132-X/$2.95
___ THE GUNSMITH #94: THE STAGECOACH THIEVES	0-515-10156-7/$2.95
___ THE GUNSMITH #95: JUDGMENT AT FIRECREEK	0-515-10176-1/$2.95
___ THE GUNSMITH #96: DEAD MAN'S JURY	0-515-10195-8/$2.95
___ THE GUNSMITH #97: HANDS OF THE STRANGLER	0-515-10215-6/$2.95
___ THE GUNSMITH #98: NEVADA DEATH TRAP	0-515-10243-1/$2.95
___ THE GUNSMITH #99: WAGON TRAIN TO HELL	0-515-10272-5/$2.95

Check book(s). Fill out coupon. Send to:

BERKLEY PUBLISHING GROUP
390 Murray Hill Pkwy., Dept. B
East Rutherford, NJ 07073

NAME_____

ADDRESS_____

CITY_____

STATE_____ZIP_____

PLEASE ALLOW 6 WEEKS FOR DELIVERY.
PRICES ARE SUBJECT TO CHANGE
WITHOUT NOTICE.

POSTAGE AND HANDLING:
$1.00 for one book, 25¢ for each additional. Do not exceed $3.50.

BOOK TOTAL $ _____

POSTAGE & HANDLING $ _____

APPLICABLE SALES TAX $ _____
(CA, NJ, NY, PA)

TOTAL AMOUNT DUE $ _____

PAYABLE IN US FUNDS.
(No cash orders accepted.)

206a

**A brand new Texas family saga
for fans of Louis L'Amour's Sacketts!**

BAD NEWS

★Giles Tippette★

Justa Williams, a bold young Texan, has a golden future ahead of him on his family's ranch—until he finds himself trapped in the tough town of Bandera, wrongly accused of murder.

But Bandera's townfolk don't know Justa's two brothers. One's as smart as the other is wild—and they're gonna tear the town apart to get at whoever set up their kin!

Look for more adventures featuring the hard-fighting Williams family—coming soon!

__ BAD NEWS   0-515-10104-4/$3.95

Check book(s). Fill out coupon. Send to:

BERKLEY PUBLISHING GROUP
390 Murray Hill Pkwy., Dept. B
East Rutherford, NJ 07073

NAME_____

ADDRESS_____

CITY_____

STATE_____ ZIP _____

**PLEASE ALLOW 6 WEEKS FOR DELIVERY.
PRICES ARE SUBJECT TO CHANGE
WITHOUT NOTICE.**

POSTAGE AND HANDLING:
$1.00 for one book, 25¢ for each additional. Do not exceed $3.50.

BOOK TOTAL	$____
POSTAGE & HANDLING	$____
APPLICABLE SALES TAX (CA, NJ, NY, PA)	$____
TOTAL AMOUNT DUE	$____

PAYABLE IN US FUNDS.
(No cash orders accepted.)